YA-F BUL
Sam Marsh and the battle
of t
Bu
94

D0393347

PL NOV 2013
VE DEC 2012
WK JUL 2013
KR AUG 2013
RU SEP 2013
WK NOV 2013

MI AUG 2014
SU JUN 2015
OS APR 2017
OS MAY 2018
CH MAY 2018

Sam Marsh and the Battle of the Cloudships

The Sam Marsh Stories - Part 2

By

Robert Bullock

Strategic Book Publishing and Rights Co.

Copyright © 2012 Robert Bullock.

All rights reserved.

No part of this book may be reproduced or transmitted in any form or by any means, graphic, electronic, or mechanical, including photocopying, recording, taping, or by any information storage retrieval system, without the permission, in writing, of the publisher.

Strategic Book Publishing and Rights Co.
12620 FM 1960, Suite A4-507
Houston, TX 77065
www.sbpra.com

To see more details of Robert Bullock's work, please visit his website, www.ninnylizard.com.

ISBN: 978-1-61897-348-1.

For Leonard Robert Bullock (Ginge) - I hope the sun is shining where you are Dad!

Acknowledgments

I wish to thank my publishers, everyone involved in the creation of this book and the supporters of my writing.

Secondly, I thank my first ever teacher, Mrs Marshall for teaching me to write! If Barbara had given up when I bit her hand on my first day at primary school you probably would not be reading this now! Barbara, I am sorry I bit you but I was only four and wanted my mum!

Thank you to my loving family of people and animals, you have always been there to keep my feet on the ground even if my head was in the clouds! Which it always will be, especially for ***Sam Marsh and the Lunar War***!

Thanks to all the children who read *Sam Marsh: The Viking King* and gave me their enthusiastic opinions on how evil Herr Krater should be!

Finally, I wish to thank my stunningly beautiful wife Kristen who has patiently stood by me and lived every word of this book every single step of the way. Kristen, there are not enough words in the world to convey how much I love you!

Contents

Excerpt - "Sam Marsh and the Lunar War"
Saturday June 13th 1943, 3.47 GMT, Lunar Mine S4D, The
Daedalus Crater, the Far side of the Moon.

Sam Marsh and the Battle of the Cloudships.

By Robert Bullock

Prologue

Sunday 16th May 1943, 2.43am, high over the island of Masoy, northern Norway

"The view is beautiful, no?" sighed Sturmbannfuhrer Eric Krater, as he and his trusty technicians stood in the 'long viking ship' shaped basket undercarriage of the immense zeppelin they used for their experiments.

"Ja, beautiful, Sir," replied Professor Klaus Jahnke, his trusty sidekick, as he peered down through powerful binoculars at the still ocean ten thousand feet below them.

Even though it was still in the wee small hours of the new day, this far north there was barely any darkness as the year fast approached midsummer. They were close to the North Pole and soon it would be daylight for twenty four hours each day.

The Sturmbannfuhrer, an eminent professor of physics from Berlin's oldest university, the Humboldt, had hastily commissioned today's early morning test flight as soon as he'd become aware of the location the Royal Navy's new 'V' Class submarine, HMS Viper, which was encroaching on his top secret testing facilities at Havoysund, near the Northern Cape, the very northern pinnacle of mainland Europe before the North Pole.

"There, there!" yelled the normally implacable Jahnke excitedly, pointing with his spare hand, "The boat is there!"

"Where? Oh ja, now I see the periscope!" replied Krater.

"She is surfacing!"

"Order the 'Death Angels' to descend at once!" shouted Krater.

"Aye Sir!" replied Jahnke, reaching for a radio, "Death Angels, DESCEND!"

Within seconds a dozen commando type soldiers, in effervescent white suites and white capes, leapt out of the basket and dived down like falcons towards their prey, the surfacing boat.

The men dived like bullets from a gun. Although they were wearing no parachutes they showed no fear. They didn't need to, they were flying like birds and had bird like flight control too. As they neared their prey they effortlessly changed their body positions from dive to flat. Their suits seamed to break their descent in an instant. This allowed them to float down and land on the sub's deck as silently as if they were feathers.

HMS Viper had surfaced. Straight away the 'Death Angels' got to work, clipping powerful limpet mines at key points all around her sleek hull.

Nobody on board knew they were even there until the hatch on the tower opened and an oily seaman poked his head out to take his first breath in four days.

"Oy!" He yelled at the men in white, "What in Heaven's name are you lot doing? Chief! Chief! There some men on the deck!"

Without uttering a single word the angels rose majestically. But their ascent was cut devastatingly short as when they'd reached only fifty feet the mines detonated early.

The explosions were vicious and deadly. Within a second the smooth, majestic hull of the Royal Navy's pride and joy was blasted into a million pieces and all the 'Death Angels' were blown to Heaven.

"Drat!" said Jahnke who reeled backwards from the shock of it all, "I knew the time settings were too short on those mines! I knew it! Those poor men."

"Ah," grinned Krater philosophically, "never mind, maybe we'll just give them longer settings next time." He smiled at Jahnke. "Actually," he said, grabbing his shoulders, "I think we can safely say that today's test flight of the flying suit was a real success, Jahnke my friend."

"Success?" snorted Jahnke, "but we have lost twelve of our best men, Herr Sturmbannfuhrer?"

"Pfff! They died for our cause. Viper is no longer a pest...and we now know that the suits work," smiled Krater coldly, "I would say that was a resounding success, wouldn't you?"

Chapter 1

Sunday 1st January 2012, 1am (GMT),
International Space Centre, 173 Miles above the
Earth.

O f the six person crew currently living and working in the cramped conditions of the International Space Centre, only one was currently on duty, the American Astronaut, Spug Wilson.

One hour earlier Spug had enjoyed a glass of vintage French champagne as Greenwich Mean Time, London Time, celebrated New Year. In three more hours he would celebrate the New Year with his home city of New York. That was the beauty of being in space, you were travelling around the Earth so fast that you could choose which of the New Year's celebrations you wanted to enjoy! And, if you were like Spug, who enjoyed a tipple now and again, you could celebrate more than once! Well Spug's excuse was that the bottle of expensive Tattinger would go flat if he left it for another day!

The bottles had been sent up especially by the French Champagne maker in specially designed lightweight plastic bottles. Heavy things could not be brought up into space. Tattinger had spent months perfecting their bottle which was, in effect, a fancy coke bottle with a special straw in the top!

For the next few minutes though, Spug's quiet revelry would

be put on hold as he went through the complicated hourly check of all the systems. The systems that kept the crew of this international space laboratory alive and well whilst zooming around mother Earth at 17,239.2 miles per hour. In fact, although it seemed like the space station wasn't moving at all it was actually travelling around the planet every 91 minutes!

A glorified science lab floating around the Earth, the space centre was the result of a long term collaboration of dozens of countries from around the globe. On board with Wilson were two Americans, two Russians, a German and a Norwegian. Yet this fact was due to change in three days' time, when three of the crew, including Spug, plunged back down to Earth and were to be replaced with one new Astronaut and two more scientists.

Because Spug Wilson was American he had to report directly to his country's control centre, the NASA (The National Aeronautics and Space Administration) Mission Control Centre, which was located at the Lyndon B. Johnson Space Centre, in Houston, Texas, in the south west of the United States.

"Houston," said Spug into the radio at precisely 1am GMT, "this is the International Space Centre, do you read me? Over."

"Reading you loud and clear Spug," replied a friendly voice from home, "how's that Tattinger going down up there Spug, over?"

"Really good! I forgot what bubbles felt like! Over." replied Spug, taking another sip from the special bottle.

Being in space, any liquids placed in a normal container would float around like solid form if not contained. Many of the normal activities of life were difficult because of the zero gravity in space.

"How's everything looking up there this fine December evening? Over." It was still 2011 back down in Houston.

"Well it's actually 2012 with me! But I can report that everything is working correctly. Over," replied Spug cheerfully, "I can also safely say that Mother Earth is looking particularly beautiful tonight, yet again! Over."

"Boy I wish I could see the view you're looking at. Over," replied Pete Courtney, the voice from Houston.

"I sure wish all the world could see it too, Pete. Over."

"In my dreams, Spug, in my dreams! Over. Speak to you in an hour, all being well. Over."

"Sure thing! Over and out."

As he signed off Spug didn't notice but there was an unusual, faint hiss on the radio. Down in Houston Pete Courtney didn't notice the hiss either because it was so faint. And neither of them had a clue that the radio connection between Earth and the International Space Centre had just been severed.

As Spug sat back and stretched out in his chair suddenly the altimeter of the station started acting strangely. It was saying that they were losing height, and fast!

That's strange! thought the Astronaut. Spug had been into space on half a dozen occasions; he was a veteran. He'd never seen anything like this before.

The pilot tapped the gauge to see if it was some kind of computer glitch or something but the numbers just kept on going down and down and with increasing speed! The meter was saying that they were dropping back to Earth! Like a stone!

Spug started to sweat and panic gripped him.

Deep breath, he thought, *take a deep breath, all this is probably some kind of software problem, after all it doesn't feel like we're dropping back to Earth does it? Then again would I feel anything so high up? Sure I would! We'd all feel it!*

The altitude gauge was dropping faster and faster. They *were* falling back to Earth, but none of the other controls were giving any kind of warning at all.

This is weird! Spug knew that all the controls should be going crazy if anything like this was happening.

He had to do something though. If they were dropping they could turn into a smouldering molten comet in seconds!

Wilson smashed his palm onto the big red 'Alert' button, which would wake the rest of the crew to this impending disaster. Nothing happened, the control was dead. **Smash!** He hit it again. Nothing! **Smash! Smash! Smash!** Harder and harder Spug hit the button but nothing happened. He tried to key into the master computer but all he got was an 'Access denied' response. Again, he tried again, but still the same response!

Spug Wilson was powerless, he couldn't do a single thing, the station was going to crash back down to Earth and there was nothing he could do to stop it.

"HELP!" Spug panicked and started screaming at the top of his voice "HEL..." His screams were cut short as light flooded through the small reinforced windows of the station into the control centre.

Bright, white light, like someone was outside pointing the biggest, most powerful, bright light right through the windows flooded in.

"What the?" mumbled Spug, "...is this what Heaven looks like?"

Automatically the astronaut looked down at the altimeter. It was still dropping and even faster now.

We're burning up! he thought, *we're burning up in the Earth's atmosphere and this is what it feels like to be burnt to a cinder coming back down to Earth? But it's not getting hot and the air con is working normally. Weird! I must be dead!"*

Without thinking Spug fastened the seat belt on his chair. *What?* He shook his head. *Why am I fastening my seatbelt?* he thought, *what good is a seat belt going to be to you? You idiot, you're dead or dying because you're crashing back to Earth, you're gonna be fried alive in a few minutes and you put your seatbelt on! What a total meathead!*

If anything the light shining into the control room got even brighter as the space station continued to plummet back to Earth.

Should I tell everyone else? he thought. *No, why disturb them, let them sleep, it's gonna be painless that way.* He decided.

THUD!

Spug was jolted out of his day dream with a case of severe whiplash and looked down at the altimeter, it had stopped! Stopped at 150 thousand feet above the Earth!

"What on Ea..."

The station had stopped dropping from the sky, stopped dropping from space, just like that, no slowing down, no deceleration, nothing, just a thud and she'd stopped stock still!

As Spug sat he was suddenly rocked backwards in his chair. They were moving again! But this time they weren't moving down towards the surface of the planet, they were moving forwards. Very, very slowly, almost purposefully....like they were being pushed!

The station moved slowly forwards for what seemed like an absolute age, yet when Spug checked his watch, which he did from time to time he discovered it was just for about four and a half minutes.

THUD! Another jolt and they stopped moving forward. They were really still now, stock still.

Knock, knock! There was a tapping sound!

What? Spug looked all around.

It sounded like it was coming from outside the centre. Something was rapping on the outside of the centre!

Knock, knock! There it was again.

And it wasn't just coming from outside the centre, it was coming from outside the window of the control room!

Spug stared in disbelief! *Knock, knock!* It was a hand! He could see a hand! *Knock, knock!* A bare hand was rapping on the window!

"Hallo!" Someone was shouting now, "Guten Tag! Hallo! Hallo! Sprechen sie Deutsche?"

Then a face appeared at the window! A man's face, a chubby

white face with red cheeks and an enormous moustache on the front like a pet black rat, but without the tail!

Spug Wilson thought he was definitely dreaming! So he closed his eyes tight shut and shook his head hard!

"Hallo bitte!" The man called again.

Wilson opened his eyes again and the face was still there! And now he was smiling, but not just smiling a little, the oddball was grinning like a Cheshire cat!

Chapter 2

Herr Krater's revenge

"**L**ook!" called Sam's Gran Freyer Becken, pointing out to sea. She had a terrified look in her eyes.

"Oh no! There are more of them coming!" yelled Sam's friend, Jenny James. Staring out from the burning embers of the Royal Villa in Svolvaer.

"The battle's not over yet men!" Admiral Stig Berg called out to his MJK soldiers and everyone else at the smouldering bomb site which had just been subjected to a brutal attack by the laser firing spider tanks of Herr Krater. "Everyone take cover again! Back down into the bunkers!"

Everyone stared in horror as the sea started bubbling and boiling once again. But no one could have ever imagined what was coming next. One by one flat metal discs plopped to the surface of the sea. There were ten discs, each five metres across.

After a few seconds of total inactivity the discs started flashing fiery red and yellow light from their edges and then they started to spin. They started turning slowly but soon were turning quicker than helicopter propellers. "No!" shouted Sam, rushing up to the front line, "it can't be!"

"What are they Sam?" asked Stig, watching in disbelief. After figuring out how to destroy the Spider Tanks, Admiral Stig Berg had learnt to trust Sam Marsh's judgement one hundred per cent.

"Spinners!" replied Sam, "They're here to finish us off!"

Everyone stood in silent terror as the Spinners turned faster and faster on the surface of the ocean. They were creating huge, violent waves. In a blinding flash of light they were airborne and moving slowly and purposefully towards the villa.

"What can we do Sam?" Even Admiral Stig was at a loss as to what to do.

Sam was about to speak when there was a gentle tapping on his shoulder. As he turned, all he saw was a long thin metal body and he had to crane his neck to see the head which was over a metre and a half above his head!

"Zebedee!" uttered a stunned Sam, "How did you get out of my workshop, and..." Sam stared behind the Robodiver, "...where did *they* all come from?"

Behind Zebedee were at least a hundred other tall, skinny android robodivers, all standing firmly to attention and demanding what they should do next from their commanding officer, Sam Marsh!

"You built them Sir," replied Zebedee, "don't you recall? And now we are here to obey your orders."

"Orders?" Sam was stunned, he didn't remember building a hundred robodivers! This felt like a dream, so he pinched himself hard.

"Ow!" He yelped.

"Sam!" Admiral Stig Berg's voice snapped Sam out of his daze.

"Yeah?"

"Sam, look!" Stig was pointing.

The Spinners had almost reached land now and it was obvious what they would do next, pretty much destroy everyone and everything. Well, except for the canister that contained Herr

Krater's precious plans, plans that he'd sent his Spider Tanks to recover in the first place.

Thinking quickly Sam rushed and grabbed the steel canister that was lying on the wet grass and held it aloft. He cleared his throat and began to shout up at the Spinners. He knew this was risky but his choices were severely limited!

"Don't come any closer Grandfather or I will destroy the plans!"

The Spinners seemed to ignore Sam and just kept coming.

"I am not joking!" Sam tried to sound as brave as he could but inside he was terrified. If his plan went wrong everyone around him would die.

"Last warning Grandfather!"

Suddenly the Spinners stopped moving forward and just hovered fifty metres above the ground.

"Ha! I knew you were listening!" shouted Sam bravely.

"Sam! No!" called Freyer, "He's pure evil! You can't bargain with a man like him! He'll kill you!"

"Sam Marsh!" boomed a voice from the Spinners.

"Grandfather!" replied Sam.

"You can't bargain with me Sam Marsh!"

"I'm warning you! I'll destroy the plans!"

"Ha! Ha! Ha! You can't even open the canister child!" snorted Krater.

"Don't bet on it!"

"Terminate them!" Krater ordered abruptly and once again the spinners started moving forward again, this time they started charging their primary weapons in readiness for the annihilation that was to follow.

Before he could do anything there was another tap on Sam's shoulder. Sam turned to find Zebedee and his battalion at action stations and they were now all heavily armed with huge laser canons.

"My men are ready Sir!" reported Zebedee "May I suggest all humans take cover immediately!"

9

"Everyone take cover!" shouted Sam.

"Take cover everyone!" repeated Stig.

Everyone except Sam, Stig and the robodivers ran for the shelter of the bunkers. Sam picked his crash helmet up from the ground and stuck it firmly onto his head and pulled the visor down. Stig did the same with his hard hat and goggles before throwing a bullet proof vest at Sam.

"Put this on Sam, it might help," he added.

"Engage the enemy robots!" ordered Sam.

Like well drilled infantrymen the robots split into ten equal groups, some remaining on the land and others diving into the sea and ripping though the waves at breakneck speed. There were ten soldiers for each Spinner and as the deep droning of the aircraft got louder the infantry got into position and readied themselves for battle.

"Fire just as the primary weapon is engaged!" bellowed Sam over his radio.

"Aye Sir!" replied Zebedee.

The robodivers quickly armed their laser canons and then waited patiently. Then the heavy droning that was coming from the Spinners stopped and a small opening on the undersides of the craft appeared.

"Wait!" shouted Sam, "Wait...FIRE!"

Sam's robot soldiers opened up with everything they had. One hundred high powered laser canons blasted upwards from the ground at exactly the same time! Their aim was perfect and they all hit their targets, the weak spot, with total precision.

There was a two second delay that felt like a lifetime and then the all the lights of the Spinners blacked out. The Spinners stopped turning. Then another two seconds later the skies over the Royal residence became a white hot inferno. Explosion after explosion rocked the clouds above the rocky islands.

The powerful blasts knocked Sam clean off his feet, his

helmet flew off and his face was quickly covered in hot sticky liquid. It was soaking right into his skin, in fact it felt like someone was rubbing it in to his face.

"Sam! Sam!" A voice was calling to Sam as he struggled to stop the rubbing.

"Sam!"

"What?" he murmured.

"Sam, wake up! It's the first of January! Happy new year mate!"

As the rubbing continued Sam opened one eye. A huge face was right next to his, a long pointed face, and it was licking him.

"Err! Gerroff!" moaned Sam, pushing the big black greyhound that belonged to Alfie Blom away.

"Ha-ha! You were shouting in your sleep Sam," muttered Spike, pulling the dog off his friend. "Come on, get up, it's a beautiful morning! We've got Zebedee to work on!"

Chapter 3

Sunday 1st January 2012, 9.15. Cloudbase 1, 80,000 feet above the North Sea, 50 miles from the Lincolnshire, England coast.

The massive flight deck that was slung below Cloudbase 2 was a hive of frantic activity. Over five hundred metres long and one hundred and fifty metres wide, its operational flight deck was almost twice as large as the United States Navy's huge aircraft carriers. However, this aircraft carrier was floating fifteen miles out on the edge of the Earth's atmosphere, almost on the edge of space itself.

Although immense, thanks to the advanced technology of The Company, this floating fortress was completely invisible to the world's radar and satellite surveillance systems. She was almost invisible except to the naked eye and who would be flying this high up or higher? Not the International Space Centre, anymore!

For the last two days she had been sat, patiently waiting for her orders, then early this morning they had come. She had performed perfectly and now her valuable prize was carefully stowed well away from the flight deck in one of its immense storage areas.

Dick Benz was a senior flight engineer on board Cloudbase 2. Dick was fifty years old, short with an unruly mop of black hair, a large moustache the size of a broom head across his upper lip and a huge pot belly that made him look like he was expecting a baby! Twins! This morning, Benz was rushing around making preparations and for the last few minutes he had been having great difficulty making one of the Skelibots understand what he was trying to say to him. The Skelibots were brilliant yet temperamental pilot droids. Normally he was a good natured man but now his patience was rapidly running out with the Skilibot pilot.

These Skelibots, human sized skeleton robots, were renowned for their bad tempers but as the discussion progressed into an argument the pilot was just squealing louder and louder, to the point where the sound was just too high for any human to even hear.

"Siggi!" shouted Dick to an interpreter, beckoning him with his one free hand (his other was clamped over his ear protecting it from the noise), "Over here a minute please Siggi before I decide to use this fellow as spare parts for my model railway!"

"EEEEEE!" Squealed the pilot, the pitch coming down to human level, probably about the breaking glass level.

"Yeah right, you understood that then?" smirked Benz as the diminutive Siggi arrived, "Bolt head!"

"EEEEEE!" squealed the pilot again. Now he was edging towards Dick holding up his gleaming metal fists ready to punch the engineer on the moustache. Things could get nasty. Dick would probably come off worse!

"What's the problem Sir?" said Siggi rushing over, holding his hands up in a calming manner at the strange, sinister looking robot that literally was just a metal skeleton. You could even see straight through him!

"I'm just trying to tell this idiot that there's a possible problem with one of the lasers on his Spinner, that's all!" said an irate Benz, "Nothing too difficult with that you wouldn't have thought!"

"EEEEEEE!" squealed the pilot again, this time at Siggi,

13

though his piercing red eyes never stopped staring at Benz, "EEEEEEEEEE! EEEEEEEEEE!"

He was shouting at the interpreter in his language which only very few humans had learnt to understand.

"What?" replied Siggi, "He said what?" He had a horrified look on his face, he then turned to the fat man with the outrageous facial hair. "Did you actually say you were going to use him for spare parts?" asked the interpreter accusingly. He was now standing with his hands on his hips.

"Err," Benz was really quite sheepish now, looking down at the ground, avoiding eye contact. He started shuffling his feet nervously, "...err."

"Dick?"

"Err, well, err, I, err, I might have done," he mumbled slowly.

"They're very sensitive you know. More sensitive than you or I! Herr Krater designed these Skelibots personally you know, and he takes great interest in them!"

"Hey! I don't even know why he bothers with robots! Why can't we have people flying those things," said Dick pointing at large flat saucer that was covered with a large cloth.

"Now listen to me Dick Benz! You know as well as me that Herr Krater is very interested in artificial intelligence and that he designs all his robots for a specific purpose. These Skelibots were designed to be the best pilots on the planet, the best reactions, the best tactical brains, the best fliers the world has ever seen. And they are the best Mr Benz, they will shortly risk their lives for the cause and I think they deserve some respect!"

"Mmm," mumbled Benz shuffling on the spot, his hands firmly stuffed into the pockets of his overalls, "maybe they are, I've still to be convinced, I have...and let me tell you, I'm not the only one!"

"I'm afraid your, or anyone else's opinions do not count!" said Siggi firmly, "and to be quite honest some humans not a million miles from me would not fit in to the Spinners!"

14

"There's no need for that kind of talk!" blurted a shocked Benz.

"Now, should I report this incident to Herr Krater, Mr Benz?"

"No, no!" snapped Dick Benz, before adding, "no need for that Siggi, no, it's just a misunderstanding," pleaded Benz, "so if you'll just tell the pilot here about the possible glitch with the laser, I think we'll leave it that shall we?" Dick held out his hand to shake the Skelibot's skeletal mitt.

"Eeee, eeee, eeee!" squealed Siggi, translating, though he knew the robot could understand English perfectly.

Reluctantly the pilot held out a hand and shook Dick's oily hand before picking up a long black cape and throwing it over its skinny shoulders and skull.

Chapter 4

Sunday 1st January 2012, 10.15am. Sam Marsh's workshop, the Royal Villa, Svolvaer.

"How are you feeling, now?" asked Sam Marsh, who was an inventor, to his latest project.

"All my circuits are regenerating perfectly, Sir," replied a metallic voice that had just been reprogrammed to speak English and not German.

"I've just got one more diagnostic to run and then he's all yours Sammy boy," added a chipper Spike Williams.

Spike had just got back from a two week work experience stint on the American aircraft carrier, USS Theodore Roosevelt, with its commander Admiral Jim Gordon.

"Where's Jenny at?" he muttered, looking up.

"Gone to Vienna with Oldemor, I think," replied Sam, who was engrossed in tinkering.

"To Vienna? As in Vienna, Austria?" said Spike.

"Your geography's improving!" noted Sam.

"It's got to Sammy my boy!" grinned Spike, who was also known as Mop, "US navy insist that I work hard at my studies, and not just computers!"

"That's good."

"It is in Austria isn't it?" added Spike, suddenly feeling unsure of himself.

"Yeah, don't know of any others," said Sam.

"Why?" Spike asked.

"Why what?" said Sam staring at his friend.

"Why's she gone to Vienna?"

"The New Year's Day concert I think," mumbled Sam.

"Concert?" Spike's ear pricked up and he suddenly sounded interested, he was into live music, "Who's playing?"

"Derr!" mocked Sam., "The Vienna Orchestra!"

"Orchestra? Orchestra?" said Spike twisting his face.

"Yeah!"

"Err! That means she's gone to a classical concert?" Spike couldn't quite believe what he was hearing. Spike Williams did not get classical music at all or the people who liked it. He liked altogether noisier, tuneless music, which he liked to play mega loud.

"Yeah, why not?" said Sam, who really wasn't bothered about music at all.

"'Cos classical music is MINGIN! THAT IS WHY NOT!" Spike was on a roll now.

"Well, Jenny obviously doesn't think so!" leered Sam.

"Urgh! What *is* the world coming too?" mumbled Spike, shaking his head which was altogether more shorn than normal.

Mop used to have his hair in an unruly wild blond mop, in fact 'Mop' had become his nickname because of his hair style, which wasn't really a style at all, just more of a bushy mound. But long hair wasn't allowed in the US Navy so he'd had to have it all unceremoniously cut off before he was even allowed to start his work placement. Normally Spike would never have had his hair cut, but working with the US Navy was a dream of his.

"Is everyone else still sleeping?" said Spike, changing the subject.

17

"What? Sleeping? Yeah, I think so," replied Sam, who was concentrating.

New Year's Eve had seen a huge party held at the Royal Villa to usher in the New Year, a large marquee had been built in the large snowy garden and lots of people from all over the islands had come to enjoy the food and dancing. Celebrating the New Year is very popular in Norway, and because of all the upheaval of the last few months everyone took advantage of the opportunity to really let their hair down for a few hours. There were massive fireworks and trips around the islands on carriages pulled by reindeer.

Sam's friends, Spike and Jenny James, who used to live with Sam in their foster home at 22 Grimwith Crescent, Holmford, had come back over to visit from England for Christmas and New Year.

And all of Sam's Great Grandma's ('Oldemor' in Norwegian or Freyer Becken to those who were not related) friends from the small town of Skreia, where she used to live, hundreds of miles away in Oppland County had come up in two coaches for the festivities too.

"Done!" said Spike triumphantly.

"Great!" said Sam jumping to his feet, "Fancy a quick dip Zebedee?"

Zebedee was Sam's name for his latest invention, well he hadn't actually invented Zebedee, he and Spike had just rebuilt him because Zebedee was a Robodiver. He was the one the Norwegian Special Forces soldiers had brought back with them when they'd been diving above the Rost Reef just before they'd had the mighty battle with the forces of Herr Krater, the head of The Company. Herr Krater was a super powerful, mega rich and cruelly ruthless man who wanted to rule the world, a man that Sam had discovered was in actual fact his great Grandfather.

"Affirmative. My joints would very much appreciate a swim, Sir," replied Zebedee, who sounded a bit weary.

"Why? Have they seized up?" asked a worried Sam.

"Negative, but movement will allow the flexible inner joint components to regenerate," replied the robot.

"Your joints *regenerate*?" Sam was gobsmacked at what he was hearing.

"Regenerate? But you're just a robot," mumbled a confused Spike.

"Negative, not a robot, Master Spike, Zebedee is AI," replied Zebedee.

"AI. Yeah right." said Spike.

"Artificial Intelligence," replied Sam, who was suddenly gripped with fear.

So, his Grandfather wasn't just developing robots, mindless machines to do his evil bidding, instead he was creating computerised people, with bodies that could heal, and maybe with intellects that could learn! At that moment Sam Marsh wondered what his Grandfather was up to at that particular moment and where he was doing it.

"Err hum," Zebedee cleared his throat, trying to grab Sam's attention.

"And *where* did you learn to do that?" replied a stunned Sam. He'd never ever thought a robot would clear his throat to get attention! That was *so* human!

"From you Sir...err, you mentioned a swim. May Zebedee take a swim Sir? And would Sirs like to accompany Zebedee?"

Sam and Spike looked at each other, and then both grinned.

"Yeah!" they yelled.

Quick as a flash they both disappeared into the large store room that was attached to Sam's workshop and reappeared a few minutes later with their diving gear. Quickly they climbed into their high tech special forces diving suits and then they helped Zebedee to his feet. His joints were really stiff and it took them a while to pull him fully upright.

As a Robodiver, Zebedee was really tall, almost seven feet tall in fact, he was extremely long and thin. Robodivers weren't built for walking around in people's houses. Zebedee would never fit through normal sized doors and would be constantly banging his head! But he was ideally suited to being fired from the narrow torpedo tubes of submarines at great speeds!

Zebedee stretched and yawned as if trying to wake himself up and then slowly followed the boys towards the exit.

Chapter 5

Sunday 1st January 2012, 5.20am local (EST) time, approaching General Edward Lawrence Logan International Airport, Boston, USA at 39,000 feet altitude.

"Flight 326 to Logan, come in Logan!" said a posh female British voice over the radio.

"We can hear you loud and clear Flight 326, Happy New Year!" replied the male American Air Traffic controller.

"And Happy New Year to you too!"

Flight 326 from London Heathrow, to Boston, Massachusetts, USA, was nearing the end of its six and a quarter, 3300 mile journey across the Atlantic Ocean. It had just been given permission by US Air Traffic Control to proceed towards descent to land on American soil.

As usual, the brand new, gigantic British Airways Airbus 380, was full to capacity with 555 people on board, most of them eager to enjoy the hospitality of New England and the north eastern states in winter time.

As was normal procedure for commercial flights, the co-pilot, Captain Jane Hughes, was in charge of landing the plane as the pilot, Captain Sean Macintyre, looked on and offered advice in a purely supervisory capacity.

"Thank you Logan, looking forward to seeing you shortly. Over," said Hughes as she prepared to bring the huge plane in to land.

"Have I asked you what you got for Christmas, Jane?" said Macintyre, casually changing the subject. Both pilots had years of experience under their belts and flying a large jet was like driving a car to them.

"No, just a few smellies, oh, and a nice new watch from Paul."

"Can't beat a nice watch, that's what I always say," replied the Captain, looking outside.

"No, it's a really nice one too, it's a Rolex."

"What? A Roley? Very nice choice! Your husband must have excellent taste," laughed the Pilot.

"Well, he did choose me!" replied Hughes laughing.

"That's what I meant!"

"What about you? What did you get, Sean?" asked Hughes.

"Err, oh yes, tickets to see the fourth Ashes test in Brisbane."

"Very nice. When are you going to Oz then?"

"Err, the end of next week."

"It's good when you can combine work and pleasure." said Hughes, studying her controls as she started the plane on its downward arc towards Boston Airport.

"Well it certainly saves on having to take leave."

"WHOAH!" yelled Hughes. As she had slowly lowered the nose of the immense passenger plane something had produced a massive amount of uplift on the jet stopping the descent dead in its tracks.

"WHAT? WHAT'S THE MATTER?" yelled a worried Captain Macintyre.

"I don't know! There was just a massive surge of uplift!"

"Uplift? Could just be turbulence?" Macintyre was trying to keep calm and assess the situation.

"No, it's not turbulence Sean, it's not variable, it's not bouncing us around it's pulling us up! Straight up!"

"Pulling?" The Pilot couldn't quite believe what he was hearing, "What do you mean pulling?"

"The controls!" yelled Hughes not answering as something else had happened, "Now even they don't seem to be working!"

"Not working, here, let me take the helm!"

Macintyre confidently took the controls from Hughes and tried desperately to regain control but he had no luck either. The plane was out of control.

"SEE!" cried Hughes overcome with anguish.

"I don't understand, I'm ordering descent but we're gaining altitude, not losing it!"

Sweat was running down the pilots face.

"We're climbing fast," reported the co-pilot, "44, 000. We're over our flight ceiling now Sean, we can't go much higher, 46, 48, 50, this is *too* high!"

None of the passengers noticed anything was the matter at all with Flight 326 and to them everything was completely in order. The pilots hadn't yet given the landing instructions to the passengers and the plane was climbing gradually and smoothly, higher and higher.

But as well as climbing she was also changing direction. Instead of heading south east down towards Logan and the American coast, she was now heading south west and back out to sea.

"What? We're changing direction now!" said Captain Macintyre, who was red faced and sweating with the exertion of fighting the controls.

"Yes, to a south westerly course," confirmed Hughes.

"We're going back out over the Atlantic." The Captain called over his shoulder to the third member of the flight crew, George Sands, their navigation and communications officer, who was desperately trying to get a signal using the emergency radio, "Radio Logan, George, tell them we've got a big problem!"

"What kind of a problem should I say, Sir?"

"Your guess is as good as mine!"

"This is Flight 362 from Heathrow, come in Logan," said Sands immediately following orders.

There was total silence. The radio was dead.

"Repeat, come in Logan. This is Flight 362 from Heathrow, come in Logan!" said Sands again.

Silence.

"There seems to be a problem with radio communications Sir," reported Sands.

"What kind of problem?" replied the Pilot.

"A big one Sir! We don't seem to have any radio at all! Everything's dead! All the electronic communications, everything, dead as a dodo..."

Just as Sands was finishing speaking the entire cockpit filled with light. Immense, blinding, white light.

In the passenger compartments, everyone sat in silence as both of the decks of the Airbus, the largest passenger plane in the world, also filled with blinding light.

Then a high pitch siren started wailing, making everyone cover their ears. It wasn't too loud but it was just so piercing. So piercing in fact that nobody could think straight through its wail. Within seconds the flight attendants collapsed and one by one every single one of the passengers blacked out and fell over too.

In the cockpit the three flight crew also fainted and slumped in their places.

Outside the Airbus, huge powerful energy clamps locked onto the wings and fuselage of the jet. Bit by bit the power to the engines was stopped. Then slowly, very slowly, so as not to damage the valuable prize, the 72 metre long plane, with its 80 metre wide wings was sucked up into a vast hold.

Chapter 6

Very few fishermen were crazy enough to put out to sea during early January from Yarmouth, Nova Scotia, for fear of the terrible icy storms that could whip up in the blink of an eye as the mild, damp air from the south west meets the cold north easterly winds coming off continental America.

But Lenny Erikson, also known affectionately as 'Leif' was no ordinary fisherman. He was a leather skinned, sea monster of a man, who had tattoos almost everywhere on his large body. He even had some gills tattooed on his almost non-existent neck. Lenny was working on fishing boats almost before he could walk and definitely before he could talk. He did most of his schooling on boats too, because his family didn't have much time for classrooms, pens and paper and books and learning stuff. In boozy bar room boasts, Lenny had long claimed that his family were direct descendants of *the* original Viking, Leif Erikson. Erikson was the tenth century Norse explorer whom it is claimed was the first European to have discovered North America, over five hundred years before Christopher Columbus claimed the continent in the name of Ferdinand and Isabella of Spain in 1492.

And like the original Erikson, Lenny was well used to battling towering waves and terrible seas that would scare even the most sea hardy of sailors.

Well renowned as a fearless man who could overcome any kind of Atlantic swell, Erikson had put out from harbour at three am this morning trying to get ahead of the opposition whilst they all slept off the New Year festivities.

The sea this morning was unnaturally calm and as Lenny opened his flask and helped himself to a cup of steaming hot coffee and a door stop sized sandwich, he sat staring at the hugeness of the ocean that he loved so much. It was so peaceful and he could see for miles and miles.

WHOOSH! The wind suddenly picked up, nearly knocking Lenny overboard. Now, all of a sudden monstrous seven metre high waves started to toss the small fishing boat violently from side to side, and up and down.

"WHAT ON EARTH!" shouted Lenny.

Then, just as he was shouting, the entire sky lit up, brighter than midday in summer. It was as bright as lightening but it wasn't a flash, it was continuous, it was like someone had flicked a light switch and then left it on! The light seemed to last for minutes and minutes and minutes. The strange bright light was illuminating the entire thrashing Atlantic Ocean as far as Lenny could see. Even with all his strength, the mighty Viking was struggling to stay on board his boat as it bounced up and down like a rubber duck in a child's bath.

As he struggled and grappled, over the noise of the wind, Lenny could hear the unmistakeable sound of jet engines high in the sky, loud jet engines, engines that sounded like a plane was either taking off or landing right on top of him. Then as quickly as the noise of the engines appeared, they disappeared, just cut out. But the light didn't go, it was still there. The blinding light was still everywhere.

Holding on for dear life Lenny struggled into the small cab of the boat and picked up the radio mic.

"Mayday! Mayday!" he yelled into it frantically.

Nothing. The radio was dead. Lenny banged the mic on the wall and tried again.

"Mayday! Mayday!" he yelled again, fear rising through his body.

Still nothing, not even a crackle of static. Just no sound at all.

Crash! A monster wave smashed against the hull of the small boat throwing Lenny right off his feet. He banged his head on the steering wheel and gashed his temple. Blood spurted everywhere. Lenny grabbed an oily rag and blotted the wound.

"What the?"

Suddenly everything felt completely different. The waves had stopped buffeting the boat. The boat was still, stock still!

Is this the eye of the storm? he thought, getting up onto his knees, holding the rag to his head and peering out of the windows.

As Lenny looked out he could see that the stormy wind was still raging but for some reason the waves had stopped buffeting the boat. Lenny slowly pulled himself to his feet with one hand and somehow managed to scramble to the edge of the boat. He peered over the side. *Good grief!* He thought.

The boat must have been one hundred feet in the air! And it was climbing higher and higher! It was being sucked into the sky!

Chapter 7

Sunday 1st January 2012, 5.30am EST, the home of the National Security Advisor, Potomac, Montgomery County, Maryland, United States.

At his large house in Potomac, Montgomery County, Maryland, just across the Potomac River from the nation's capital, Washington DC, the NSA to the President, Slim Easton was riding his stationary bike and sipping sour tomato juice as he did every morning, come rain or shine.

As always a phone wasn't far away, yet even the workaholic Easton didn't expect it to ring at this time on New Year's Day.

"Easton!" he gasped into the phone as he peddled furiously desperate to get more miles in.

"Slim, it's Jane McCoy." Jane McCoy was one of the top managers at NASA down in Houston, Texas.

"Hello Jane, what's the matter?" Easton knew something had to be the matter for Jane McCoy, the Scottish born scientist, to even consider bothering him at this hour on one of Slim Easton's rare days off.

"We've lost the International Space Centre."

"Lost, whadaya mean, lost, Jane?" he was still peddling. "Lost contact Slim..."

"Phew!" snorted the Texan, chuckling and interrupting the

scientist, "You sure got me going then Jane! For a second there I thought you lot had actually gone and lost the space centre!"

"Err, sorry Slim, I was just coming on to the rest of the news," replied McCoy in a Scottish/American accent.

"Rest of the news?" Now Easton was starting to get worried and slowed his pedalling.

"We lost contact Slim because there are satellite problems, dozens of them are going off line. I can tell you communications are becoming really difficult."

"Difficult? Off line?" Slim stopped pounding the pedals and clutched the phone to his ear.

"Yes, Sir, some satellites are becoming inoperative. Oh, there goes another one….and another!"

"What on earth are you saying, Jane?" Slim got off his bike.

"Well, I honestly don't know Sir, but I think we're headed towards some kind of major problem! And we don't have a clue why it's happening!"

Chapter 8

Sunday 1st January 2012, 10 .30am, outside Sam Marsh's workshop, the Royal Villa, Svolvaer.

A good covering of snow lay on the ground outside the spacious Royal Villa where Sam Marsh, the new chieftain of the Norwegian Lofoten Islands, lived. Even though the islands are in the Arctic Circle, as they are situated off the west coast of the country, they benefit from the warm air coming off the Atlantic and tend not to get as much snow as many other places in the country. But the Lofoten Islands in January could still be a starkly bleak and cold place to live.

It was still dark outside, this far north during winter time meant over twenty two hours of darkness each day. It wasn't complete darkness for all that time because there were grey dawns and dusks that seemed to go on and on forever.

Outside the workshop it was just dawning a steely grey, and the blackness that blanketed the countryside, the islands and the sea, was slowly and very gradually being replaced by the muted light.

Sam Marsh didn't mind the long winter nights. His life now was the best it had ever been. Six months ago he was just a foster child whom no one cared about. He lived in a sad council home at 22 Grimwith Crescent, Holmford, in northern England.

Unlike the other children in the home, Sam didn't have a history at all, he had no family and as far as he was concerned he had no future. Sam's life seemed worthless, no one wanted him and he felt he had no future. That was until last October, when his life changed forever.

Zebedee, carrying the boys' heavy air tanks, was followed by Sam and Spike as they made their way across the garden towards the cliff path which led down to the beach.

"Hey!" called a Norwegian woman's voice from behind them, "Where are you lot going?" It was Jorunn, the big, plump lady with white hair and bright red cheeks who was the housekeeper at the Royal Villa. She looked after Sam and had done ever since he'd first arrived. Jorunn was just about the first person to hug Sam. At first it felt strange but it felt nice at the same time.

"Oh Jorunn," muttered Sam.

"Ja, 'Oh Jorunn indeed young man! Where are you going with that lot?"

"Err, we thought we'd just go for a quick swim with Zebedee here," replied Sam.

"Oh did you now?"

"Please Jorunn, he's safe now," begged Sam.

"Safe? Are you sure Liten Prinsen?" replied the housekeeper. She always called Sam 'Liten Prinsen', which meant little prince in Norwegian.

"Yeah, sure, it's all safe now Jorunn, don't worry," replied Sam.

"Well OK," Jorunn replied reluctantly. Jorunn didn't like Sam to leave her sight, "Don't be long, I'm making a special Kransekake for after lunch."

"Kransekake? Well, we definitely won't be long now!" said Spike licking his lips. He loved Jorunn's cakes, especially celebration cakes like Kransekake.

Chapter 9

As the tiny fishing boat was sucked higher into the sky, Lenny Erikson thought he must be dreaming. Had he actually really got up that morning or was he still asleep in his comfy bed in his nice warm cottage? Maybe it was all the cheese he ate for his supper last night making him have a nightmare? People do say that's what happens if you eat too much.

With two of his massively thick digits he pinched himself hard.

"Ow!" he yelled, as the pain seared through his arm. It was real enough...well the pain was anyway!

Suddenly four ghostly white figures landed in front of Lenny on his grubby, fishy deck, as quiet as feathers landing on a carpet.

"Oi! What the...?" Lenny's yell was cut short as something was puffed into his face by one of the figures.

Lenny suddenly felt sleepy. His legs buckled under his weight and within a few seconds he crashed to the deck.

Chapter 10

The Kehlsteinhaus or Eagle's Nest, was situated close to the summit of the 2,444 metre high Kröndlhorn Mountain in the Austrian Alps. The high security luxurious mountain top villa was perched precariously on the rock and was extremely private. The only way to and from the residence was by the helicopter, private helicopter. Anyone, any other helicopters or aircraft risked being shot at if they strayed too close.

To the naked eye, the large five star complex looked like an exclusive luxury holiday retreat for the rich and famous. But the pristine facade masked a high tech complex that was sunk deep into the solid granite core of the mountain.

It was a bitingly cold, crisp morning and the sunlight glistened off the ice coated walls and verandas of the white buildings.

"He's coming your way Chigashev!" shouted Frolov in Russian into his radio.

"Which way is he coming from Frolov?" replied his partner in crime.

The two burly muscle men, ex weightlifting, KGB hatchet men, were wearing their 'uniform' of black leather lace up boots, black combat pants, and three quarter length black leather jackets.

As usual the hairs on their heads were cropped so closely that you could almost see their pink flaky scalps. They were both wearing designer dark glasses to help deal with the blinding glare from the sun reflecting off the snow and ice.

Chigashev and Frolov were the sort of men you hired if you wanted things, evidence, people, whatever, to disappear. But these two weren't for hire anymore because they worked for just one boss, Herr Krater. They were completely devoted to Krater and would do anything he asked without ever questioning an order.

"Round the south veranda!" said Frolov as they organised themselves.

As he positioned himself, Chigashev could hear heavy breathing coming his way as he turned the last corner. Quickly he lifted his Kalashnikov AK-103 machine gun, its stock folded to make it more pistol like so he could use it one handed. He skidded to a halt, grabbed a railing to steady himself and waited, his breath held.

At the very last minute he jumped out in front of his victim, his gun ready to fire.

"STOP!!" yelled Frolov, holding his hand up, "Don't fire!"

Just in time Chigashev checked his natural instinct to squeeze the trigger.

"Frolov? It's you!"

"For sure it's me! What are you, an idiot?"

"Where's he gone?" asked Chigashev, looking confused.

"What do you mean? He didn't pass you?" questioned Frolov.

"No way! Believe me, no one could have got past me!"

"So that means there's only one place he could have gone!"

The pair both rushed, slipping and sliding on the shot ice over to the perimeter railings and peered over. There, in the far distance a thousand feet below they saw a streak of white zooming away across the mountain valley.

Without thinking both men opened fire and let rip a couple of long blasts into the fresh air, but the chances of hitting such a fast moving target at such long range were extremely low.

Chapter 11

Sunday 1st January 2012, 10.25am, swimming around Austvågøy with a Robodiver

Kongetorsk, or King Cod, was right about the weather on Lofoten today. For over a thousand years the islands fishermen had relied upon Kongetorsk, and he was always right about the weather.

The day was turning into a freezing, crisp, winter's morning, a perfect day for a swim, perfect that is if you've got an army dry suit that is capable of keeping the freezing cold Arctic Ocean at bay. If you haven't such a suit you would freeze to death in less than ten minutes! Sam and Spike crunched down the private royal beach towards the calm sea with Zebedee.

After the battle of Lofoten, Sam had pleaded with everyone to be able to keep the Robodiver that he and Admiral Stig Berg had brought back on their rocket sofas. Eventually, Stig persuaded Slim Easton and Oldemor to allow Sam to repair the cyborg and for Spike to reprogram it to bring it back to life.

Robodivers are highly efficient swimming cyborgs that are perfectly designed to swim through the water almost as fast as a powerful torpedo. They are much taller than any standard cyborg, almost three metres tall but are very skinny. They have to be thin because they are fired into the water through standard submarine torpedo tubes.

Sam, Spike and the strange tall silver man stood on the deserted beach and prepared themselves to go out into the black foreboding waters. The boys felt tiny next to the towering android.

"Ahoy there!" someone shouted behind them.

When the boys turned around they saw the grinning face of Alfie Blom and his two black greyhound dogs walking towards them. Alfie was a weird looking man who always dressed in bright colours but the boys had discovered that his looks were highly deceptive. Blom was a retired Admiral with contacts at the highest level both in Norway and abroad.

Today Blom was wearing his trademark multi-coloured suit. The suit always made Sam think that Alfie bought normal suits and splashed multi coloured paint all over them whilst madly painting pictures. The multi coloured style wouldn't suit most people but everyone had to admit it did look good on Blom.

"Hi Alfie!" called Sam.

"Hiya!" added Spike.

"Going for a swim lads?" asked Blom as the dogs leapt up and down, their tails wagging like pendulums. They were always pleased to see Sam and Spike.

"Yeah, Jorunn said it was OK," said Sam, "we've reprogrammed Zebedee."

"Err! I've reprogrammed him!" corrected Spike.

"OK, Spike's reprogrammed him," Sam leered at his friend.

"Fine with me," shrugged Alfie, "just be careful, the water's really cold you know."

"We've got our Special Forces suits on," replied Spike.

"Even so, be careful, no technology is a replacement for good old common sense!"

"OK," they said together."

"Have you checked Kongetorsk?" Alfie Blom, like most sailors was very superstitious, the sea had to be respected he always said, conditions could change at the drop of a hat and you had always to be careful and use your common sense.

"Yeah we've checked him," said Sam.

"And?" questioned Alfie.

"He says it's set fair all day, conditions are perfect."

"Fair enough," muttered Alfie walking on, "but don't be too long, Jorunn will be making a special lunch, you won't want to miss it, especially you Spike."

"No, no," mumbled Spike, who loved his food, "we won't be long, we're just going out for a quick spin."

"Zebedee, please repeat mission rules!" questioned Sam as Alfie walked on.

"Zebedee, Sam Marsh and Spike Williams will swim together, arms interlocked at all times. We will make one circumnavigation of the island of Austvågøy and then return to this beach."

"Great!" said Sam putting the mouthpiece of his breathing apparatus in his mouth, "Are you ready Spike?" he mumbled.

"Ready!" mumbled Spike.

Sam had learnt from his friends at the Norwegian Special Forces, the MJK, that in order to stay close to colleagues on underwater missions they had to interlock arms, that way they couldn't become separated and get into a dangerous situation.

"Let's go!" murmured Sam, pulling his goggles down. Over the last couple of months Sam had become a qualified diver thanks to expert tuition from his friends over at the Ramsund Special Forces Base.

Hand in hand the three mismatched characters walked down the beach towards the sea. Sam and Spike walked uncomfortably in the huge flippers that their friend Captain Morten Rudd had given them. The Robodiver walked confidently and annoyingly easily into the water.

The beach gently shelved beneath their feet and soon Sam and Spike were up to their necks in the water. Gently, the cyborg knelt down and assumed the arm in arm swimming position. Sam gave the thumbs up to the Robodiver and suddenly they were under the water and breathing the air from the tanks.

Although the boys were kicking hard it was the thrust of the powerful robot's legs that was propelling them through the water at over fifty miles per hour.

They were soon out into the deeper water and within minutes they were swimming under the Raftsund Bridge like underwater rockets. They were heading anti- clockwise around the island.

They overtook a couple of playful Orcas who thought for a few seconds about chasing them for their lunch, before realising the futility of chasing something you could never catch!

Swimming at fifty knots under water means that you can't see very much at all, but Zebedee had inbuilt sonar as well as eyes that could see for miles through the darkness. Zebedee was in his element and they were perfectly safe.

At one point Sam signalled to his robot friend to come to the surface as they had agreed. They shot out of the water like a leaping dolphin performing tricks for a paying audience!

"Wheyhey!" the boys reeled.

Whilst they were leaping above the waves Sam and Spike could see where they were, the north side of the island. They shot passed a couple of fishing boats and waved at the bemused men who thought they were seeing things, until they recognised Sam, the new chieftain of the islands.

"Hey Sam! Good morning!" they shouted.

Sam signalled to dive deep and head out towards the Rost Reef and the wreck of the SS Helmsfjord, the ship that held the plans that Herr Krater fought so hard to recover in the battle of the Spider tanks. They speeded up and bore down into the blackness.

Spike and Sam lit powerful underwater torches and within minutes the ghostly wreck came into sight.

"Let's go inside," signalled Sam.

"Must be careful, Sir," Zebedee signalled back.

As the boys and the Robodiver climbed through a hole in the side of the boat, Sam asked Zebedee to stand guard at the entrance as it was very cramped inside the wreck.

Sam and Spike crawled carefully along the submerged passageways. Very soon they came to an ancient looking air lock. They crawled inside, shutting the door and spinning the lock until it was firmly shut.

Opening the door on the other side, water drained out. They entered a large room which looked like a laboratory. Both boys unclasped their breathing apparatus and lifted their goggles.

"What is this place?" gasped Spike looking around, his torch light casting a dim shadow over the room.

"Some kind of lab," replied Sam, "it could be my grandfather's lab."

"He can't have been on the boat when it sank though, could he, he'd be dead."

0"Sam! What is it Sam?" shouted Spike, then he saw him too.

There crouched over the table was a man, a long dead man. His lifeless body had wizened and darkened, his head all but bald, but he was still wearing a white lab coat and he still had a pen in his hand.

"Well I guess we know whose lab it was," shrugged Spike.

"Poor man," mumbled Sam as he moved closer to the body, "when the boat sank he must have been trapped in his airtight lab. He must have suffocated in here."

"Err, I don't think so Sam," said Spike, "we're breathing, so the air's fine, he must have starved or something."

"What a horrible way to die," said Sam sadly, examining the man closely, "really horrible and lonely."

"What's he writing?"

"Err," Sam looked more closely, "a diary, and, err, yeah the last bit's underlined, it's in German so I can't understand it. Do you think he'd mind if we took it?"

"I suppose he wrote the diary for someone to find it," said Spike, "come on Sam, it's creepy down here, let's go."

Sam picked up the old diary and placed it in a watertight bag. Both boys said goodbye to the scientist and went back out of the air lock.

Once out into the open ocean the team headed home via the impressive Gimsøystraumen Bridge, with its 839 metre length and 148 metre central span.

Coming back around the island towards Svolvaer they started slowing down, and then almost as quickly as they had left they were back in the shallow water of the beach at the Royal Villa.

The group surfaced and Sam took out his mouthpiece and lifted his goggles.

"Wowee!!" he yelled at the impassive Robodiver, "Next time we're going to go to the North Pole, whadaya reckon Spike!"

"Wicked!" replied Spike, "let's get inside and take a look at that diary."

Chapter 12

Sunday 1st January 2012, 11.00am, Herr Krater's study, The Kehlsteinhaus, the Kröndlhorn Mountain, Austrian Alps

"Knock, knock!" Frolov tapped quietly on the solid oak door of Herr Krater's study.

They waited a few seconds then heard a muffled "Come!" Both men gave an involuntary shiver as they edged forward. Herr Krater scared everyone, even ruthless gangsters!

Chigashev gingerly turned the heavy iron door handle and took a deep breath. Even he, a battle hardened former KGB man, was terrified of Herr Krater, a man they knew controlled great evil.

The KGB was the dreaded national security agency of the Soviet Union from 1954 until 1991 and people like Chigashev and Frolov were involved with terrible violence and subterfuge in order to protect the security of the country that is now known as Russia. KGB was once a phrase that shot fear into the hearts of people all across the world.

But even the people in charge of the KGB feared Herr Krater.

The men entered slowly, cautiously, only remembering at the last minute to take off their dark glasses as a mark of respect for the only man who would employ them at the downfall of the Soviet Union.

Respect was important to Herr Krater. Yes, respect...the last person who didn't show him it ended up walking the plank, literally, right here and found himself heading towards the bottom of the 2444 metre high Kröndlhorn Mountain without a parachute!

Aside from his cruelty, Herr Krater was well known for his bizarre sense of humour. He always thought of his mountain chalet as another of his ships. He called the various floors or levels, 'decks' and he called his staff, 'officers'. He even dined each night at the 'Captain's Table! And when the complex had been built he'd insisted on having a plank made just so no-one ever thought of challenging him.

"Well, where is the chip?" said Herr Krater calmly in perfect English.

He was sat with his back to his henchmen staring out across the fabulous mountain landscape. The office was huge and furnished like a library. On three sides floor to ceiling bookshelves lined the walls, in fact you couldn't see walls for books there were so many. The one wall not covered with books was a huge picture window. The view from it was simply stunning, a fantastic, constantly changing, snowy alpine mountain scene. It was just like real life television. Herr Krater seemed totally engrossed with the view.

"Lu has the chip, Sir," replied Frolov in a shaky voice.

"How did this happen?"

"We don't know," added Chigashev honestly. Lu worked in research and development and Chigashev and Frolov in security. Until now their paths hadn't crossed at all.

"WELL FIND OUT!" bellowed Krater without turning.

"We have launched an investigation already, Sir," replied Chigashev, his legs trembling and buckling.

"Good," Krater's manner had calmed once more, he cleared his throat and spoke again, this time quietly, "and how exactly did Lu actually escape from the complex?"

"Over the edge," said Frolov.

"Over the edge? What? You mean over the railings?"

"Yes, Sir."

"He had a parachute then?" Krater wanted details, but he already feared the worst.

"No, Sir," replied Chigashev.

"So this means he had one of my suits?"

"Yes, Sir," said Chigashev.

"Then he *must* be captured, that suit *must* be returned. Do you understand?"

"Yes, Sir," said Frolov.

"Send out the flies, NOW!"

"But he'll be on the way to Kitzbühel, or Vienna," argued Chigashev.

Frolov had his finger on his lips, trying desperately to shut his colleague up before he upset Krater.

"Then you had better MOVE!" roared Krater.

Within one minute, Chigashev and Frolov had legged it from Krater's office and ordered that the flies be despatched to retrieve Simon Lu, dead or alive.

Chapter 13

Sunday 1st January 2012, 12 noon, high above the Kitzbühel 3S Aerial Tramway, Kitzbühel, Austria.

As he flew like a human jet plane young Simon Lu looked down on the immense 3S Aerial Tramway at Kitzbühel. The 3642 metre long aerial tramway impressively bridges the huge Saukasergraben Valley and connects the world renowned skiing areas of Kirch and Resterhöhe with each other.

At 12 noon on New Year's Day, as Simon flew high overhead like a bird, each of the twenty four cabins of the tramway were full of festive skiers enjoying the fine weather and excellent skiing conditions.

Buzz, buzz! As he flew Simon heard something behind him.

Buzz, buzz! Whatever could it be up here?

Lu was wearing a special flying suit made out of a new high tech fabric and flying in one of these angel suits meant you could normally hear no flying noise apart from the sound of the air whooshing past your face as you flew along at over four hundred miles per hour. But as he'd got used to the noise Lu's hearing had adapted to the noise of the wind and his ears quite rapidly blocked out this noisy hiss of the fast moving air. This meant he could hear sounds coming up from the ground remarkably well, like he was floating in a hot air balloon.

This sound was different though, it wasn't the normal sound of air passing his face at high velocity, or something floating up from the surface of the earth. No this was a weird noise. It was coming from behind him.

What could be behind me? thought Simon.

But something definitely was behind him and the sound was getting louder and louder. Whatever it was, it was closing in! FAST!

Buzz, buzz! Buzz, buzz! There it was again! And the sound was getting really loud now. Simon couldn't imagine what it could be. Then he glanced over his shoulder and then saw them! Mechanical insects!

Closing in on him by the second was a swarm of a dozen mechanical flies. Each as big as a large family dog, their wings were a blur of rapid movement as they beat frantically. Six thin legs dangled below the fat shiny silver bodies, and on the side of the head were large bulbous eyes, each the size of a head itself! The bulging eyes were moving round and round, apparently surveying the scene all around them. They consisted of what looked like thousands of tiny moving mirrors of different colours and sizes, shimmering and reflecting the light from the sun and from the snowy ground.

Buzz, buzz! Buzz, buzz! The noise was terrible! Constantly there, it was a deep, vibrating drone, which seemed to make Simon's body vibrate. He started to feel dizzy and sick.

He had to do something. Simon changed direction, moving quickly to his right.

Buzz, buzz! Buzz, buzz! The squadron of flies followed and changed direction too.

So Simon went to his left.

Buzz, buzz! Buzz, buzz! The flies turned left too.

Simon climbed higher into the clear blue sky.

Buzz, buzz! Buzz, buzz! So did they!

It was dawning quickly on Lu that these fly robots were following him as their speed had fallen into line with his, but it was clear that they weren't closing in on him. Yet! They must be awaiting their orders!

Simon Lu was a young, twenty four year old engineering graduate from Trinity Hall College, Cambridge, England. Originally from Hong Kong, he'd boarded at Giggleswick School in North Yorkshire from being a young child, before Cambridge.

It had all started when he'd just finished the Michaelmas term in his last year at Trinity Hall, one of Cambridge's smallest but most exclusive colleges, when he'd received an intriguing email, one that he just could not ignore.

This email had at first sounded almost too good to be true. But it had indeed been true and really, really good for the last two years. Shortly after supper yesterday evening though, things start turning sour.

Now as he flew along in his high tech 'Angel' suit, Simon started to fear the worst. Although he had never seen anything like these mechanical flies in the two years that he had worked for Herr Krater and The Company in Austria, he knew that it must have been him that had sent the awful creatures that were following him. He'd heard stories of some of the other technologies The Company were developing. He'd heard tales of weird and wonderful cybernetic experiments, of fantastic robots and amazing machines. He'd heard stories about the development of artificial intelligence. No one else could have this kind of technology, not the Americans, the Chinese or the Russian, no one, only Krater.

Now he was face to face with Herr Krater's technology Lu had to try and shake it off with good old fashioned cunning. He had an idea.

Chapter 14

Thursday 17th December 2009, 11.47pm Jerwood Library, Trinity Hall, Cambridge, England. Lu's history.

It had been 17th December 2009 when Simon Lu's life had been turned upside down. It had been his life changing day. Simon had been under lots of stress in the run up to the end of term, lots of hassle from his family back home, what they wanted him to do didn't match up with what he wanted from his life.

So, after lots and lots of soul searching Simon had decided to tell his parents that he wasn't returning home to his family in Hong Kong for Christmas and New Year. Mum and Dad had been pestering him for weeks to come home, they'd even bought air tickets, but Simon hated flying in planes so much, he always felt as if someone else held the key to his destiny and he couldn't cope with that. Simon Lu was a control freak who hated it when things were out of his power. It wasn't that he didn't like flying, he actually really loved parachuting and paragliding, but when he was doing those things he was the one that was in control. But he had no control in a jet plane. And besides, at six foot five inches tall, being cramped up like a sardine in a tin didn't fill him with much joy.

So, after pleading and pleading with his parents he'd

convinced them that flying in a tin box for eighteen hours wasn't the best way of spending the run up to Christmas, especially since he had a lot of work to do if he was to pass his finals in a few months' time.

More bothered about their son getting a good degree than his physical comfort his parents had reluctantly agreed and allowed him to stay put in England.

Simon Lu breathed a sigh of relief when he finally realised that he was going to be allowed to stay at Trinity Hall and get ahead with his course work instead of going home for Christmas.

Not your usual swotty looking student, Simon wasn't typically Asian looking either, he did have the traditional dark complexion and jet black hair but he was tall and powerfully built and he was sporty. He liked to row for his college and enjoyed the occasional game of rugby.

As Simon was working on his laptop in the library, the 'You have new email' message pinged. Simon jumped as the ping dragged him out of his mind wanderings. As usual he curiously opened his inbox and there it was, a strange, mysterious message that had him hooked straight away.

"Are you interested in working for me, Simon?" was the question.

Well that's straight to the point! he thought.

"Well, I do like to be direct, Simon!"

What?

At first Simon had thought it was just a spam message, some scam that was trying to get him to divulge all his personal details and then raid his bank account of every last penny. He was just about to hit delete when the computer pinged again;

"Don't delete me Simon! I'm serious, do you want to work for The Company?"

The Company? What company? thought Simon.

"*The* Company!" pinged the email. It was if it could read his thoughts.

How did you know that's what I was thinking? he thought.

"Because we know everything!"

Everything?

"Everything!"

Like what?

"Like the fact that you're sat in the Jerwood Library, at Trinity Hall College, on seat 18b!"

"What?" Simon looked around but there was no one about, no one at all. He looked up and down, all around the large room, but there were no cameras, none anywhere. None that he could see anyway.

He checked the webcam on his computer but it was firmly turned off.

Simon looked at his computer again.

"You're wearing a blue jumper, Levi jeans, Adidas trainers that look like they're about to fall to pieces and you've got a small piece of Pizza stuck on your chin!"

What? Simon looked carefully at his reflection and there, lo and behold was a small fragment of the 'pizza fungi' that he'd gobbled down two hours before.

"How?" he said out loud.

"We know everything..."

As he sat down to read further, Simon didn't see the minute mechanical woodlouse scurry away to safety under the table.

Simon Lu was hooked!

Less than two hours later Simon was sat in a grubby all-night cafe waiting to meet Josephine, a small dark, pretty girl that he grew to know very well over the next few months. This was when things got really serious. When Simon was drawn in by The Company.

At weekends he had received text messages telling him to meet Josephine at Stansted Airport and once there they would board private jets which whisked them to offices all over Europe. For his Easter holidays he visited what he thought was The

Company's headquarters at the Kehlsteinhaus, on the Kröndlhorn Mountain in the Austrian Alps. That's when things got really interesting for Simon Lu, touring the labs and facilities of The Company.

Just before the summer term started Simon Lu signed a contract agreeing to go and work for The Company at its headquarters in the Austrian Alps when his exams were finished.

Fantastic! he thought as he digitally signed the contract, *I don't have to fly, I hate flying, I can drive!*

Chapter 15

Sunday 1st January 2012, 12.30 pm, The Royal
Villa, Svolvaer. Celebratory Lunch.

"Read this bit," urged Spike, engrossed in the diary. Spike had scanned the old foreign words into his and Sam's laptops, translated them and each of them was curiously going through it. The document was long and some parts of it contained diagrams and mathematical sums that neither of the boys understood, yet other bits were remarks and reflections.

"Mm?" mumbled Sam.

"It say's Herr Krater invented a special flying suit."

"What?" Sam's ears pricked, "Like a rocket pack or something?"

"No, no," Spike shook his head, "I don't think so, more like a special material that makes the wearer float and fly, he was fine tuning this when the Helmsfjord set sail, so says this scientist, what's his name? Hans Schwarz?"

"Yeah, that's right."

"Well, Professor Schwartz didn't know that much about it. He says they blew up a British sub though, the, err, where is it? Err, the HMS Viper."

"They blew up a British sub?" Sam was shocked.

"I suppose it was war time," replied Spike.

"Suppose."

"What are you reading Sam?"

"Err, oh, yeah, just about my grandfather. It seems that everyone was afraid Herr Krater."

"Oh," Spike shrugged his shoulders.

"No, I don't think you understand Spike, really afraid, terrified!" Sam was deadly serious, "He killed people all the time."

"Sam! Spike! Lunch!" bellowed Jorunn from the kitchen.

"Come on, come in boys!" said a busy looking Jorunn as she rushed around the kitchen preparing lunch, "Wash your hands over there and then go and sit in the dining room."

"But we've just had a shower!" protested Sam, "We're clean!"

"Wash your hands!" ordered Jorunn, holding her rolling pin up threateningly, "Or else!"

"OK, OK!" said Sam giving in, he knew Jorunn's rolling pin was a lethal weapon!

He and Spike walking into the huge dining room, its enormous oval table set out with lots of place settings. At the centre of the table was a huge cake. Jorunn had surpassed herself, it was massive! The Kransekake was the biggest cake that either Sam or Spike had ever seen, it was at least a metre tall. Ring upon ring of sponge was layered one on top of another, big ones at the bottom and small ones at the top to form a cone shape. And it was drizzled all over with sticky white icing. As usual there were dozens of little Norwegian and British flags sticking out of it. However, today Jorunn had some other flags too, little blue flags with white roses on them.

"Yorkshire flags!" called out Sam happily to Jorunn. He was proud to have been brought up in Yorkshire, "You found some Yorkshire flags!"

"Ja for sure, but it wasn't easy Sam but I'll have you know that I have contacts over in Yorkshire," replied Jorun winking at Spike, who grinned back.

"Cheers Spike!" said Sam.

"No probs, mate," replied Spike coolly.

"Who's coming today Jorunn?" asked Sam.

Just at that moment the front door opened and the two greyhounds came rushing into the dining room, licking their lips at the thought of eating the entire Kransekake!

"Out! Out! Get them out!" shrieked Jorunn, "Alfie Blom! Get them out of here! Where are you Alfie Blom! Keep your stupid dogs under control or they'll feel my rolling pin too!"

"Ja, Ja, keep your håret on woman!" laughed the multi-coloured Blom, who appeared at the door, careful to come no further.

"I'll håret you too! Alfie Blom!" spat Jorunn, whacking her rolling pin around like a sword.

"You've got to catch me first, old woman!" he laughed, leaving the room at speed.

Quickly, Sam and Spike each grabbed a dog and pulled them out of the dining room, making sure to shut the door firmly after themselves.

In the large palatial lounge were Svend and Odd, Sam Marsh's special security men and Alfie Blom. The boys let them go and immediately the dogs ran in and lay down on the rugs in front of the log burning stove. Even though the house was always warm everywhere, like all Norwegian houses, the lounge was always extra warm. And the stove was like a dog magnet! Sam and Spike flopped down on one of the huge comfy three seater sofas that surrounded the stove.

"How was your swim boys?" asked Alfie.

"Oh yeah, you were taking Zebedee out for a spin around the island weren't you?" asked Svend, the younger, slimmer, handsome and more serious of the two security men.

"Yeah that's right," replied Sam, looking at his friend "great, it was great."

"More than great, Sam," corrected Spike, grabbing his laptop from the coffee table where he'd dumped it earlier, "well wicked I'd say!"

Neither boy mentioned the diary.

"Zebedee worked OK then Sam?" asked the slightly portly Odd sipping on a cup of strong, sweet black coffee.

"Oh, yeah, perfect, really great. I'm really pleased with him," replied Sam tinkering with his iPhone.

As they sat, Jorunn brought in a tray of drinks, a pot of steaming coffee for the men and cans of Coke, Fanta and Solo for the boys. One of the dogs lazily lifted his head off the rug and had a sniff.

"Oy! You keep your dogs under control Alfie Blom!" she warned.

"Ja, sure will!" agreed Alfie, helping himself to a coffee, "Thanks."

"Oh Ja," said Jorunn, "There's another guest here Liten Prinsen."

"Hammer?" asked Sam, looking up. Hammer was the Mayor of Svolvaer, a jolly man who looked like Santa Claus. Hammer always had a story to tell and Sam liked him.

"Not Hammer. He's no guest! He's here almost every day!" snapped Jorunn, "No, someone from England, from Holmford."

Sam was suddenly very suspicious, he knew exactly where everyone he liked from England was. Spike was sat next to him, Jenny was in Vienna with Oldemor, and his social worker, Sarah Steel, was coming over to visit in a couple of days.

"SAMMY MARSH!" bellowed a strangely familiar voice. A woman's voice. One Sam hadn't heard for a few months. One he wasn't sure he wanted to hear again.

Sam froze! Suddenly he was in a blind panic. His stomach was churning and he had terrible mixed feelings. Suddenly he was transported all the way back to the bad old days when he lived at 22, Grimwith Crescent, the days when he had no past, had no history and, in a way, no future. The days when he was an orphan.

"Jessie?" questioned Sam, staring at Spike, who was

engrossed in mind melding with his laptop. Mop was completely oblivious to his surroundings. Spike didn't even bother to look up.

Thanks for the support Spike, thought Sam.

"Aren't you gonna give your old friend Jessie Brooks a big hug then, Sammy Marsh?"

Jessie Brooks, Sam's foster carer when he lived in the care home at 22, Grimwith Crescent, Holmford, England was stood in the lounge, his lounge, in his house, on his island, in his new country! He wasn't sure whether her wanted to be here.

Strangely enough although Sam's first thought was to run, to bolt and run away, well away from his past, he didn't. Something deep inside, unexpectedly made him stay, turn around and run and hug Jessie instead.

With tears in his eyes Sam flew at Jessie and hugged her hard. Jessie responded by giving Sam a massive bear hug. He never liked Jessie's bear hugs when he lived in England, yet for some reason he didn't mind them now.

"I always said you were a right clever clogs, Sam Marsh, and look, I was right! Sam Marsh super inventor! The person who saved the world! You're famous you know!"

Tears were rolling down Jessie's cheeks, and even though he tried desperately to be brave and hold them back himself they were rolling down Sam's cheeks too! He shot a glance at Spike, but he was still completely oblivious to his surroundings!

Typical!

"Jessie," mumbled Sam.

"You were always special Sam Marsh! Didn't I always say you were special?"

"I can't remember," and he honestly couldn't. Jessie used to say lots of things, most of them claptrap. But she was the only mother he had known for most of his life.

"Well, I did, you are, you're special."

Suddenly Sam pulled away and stared at Jessie, who was

blubbing like a baby. He had remembered something really important.

"The dogs? Your dogs? What's happened to them? Where are they?"

Jessie Brooks had two elderly greyhounds, who Sam loved to pieces. They were just like Alfie's dogs except a lot older and a bit doddery!

"Oh heck! Blimey! The dogs!" yelled Jessie, turning and waddling out of the door as fast as her chubby legs could carry her. Sam hated the way she was always so over dramatic, a real drama queen.

"What?" shouted a worried Sam, "What is it? What's happened to them?"

"They're outside!" shouted Jessie back.

"Oh no! Not more dogs!" groaned Jorunn, who had appeared with even more drinks and some cheesy puff nibbles, which she'd discovered were Jessie's favourite. Jorunn always made it her business to make sure she knew what everyone's favourite food was.

Sam ran to the door, easily overtaking the lumbering slow bulk of Jessie. As he opened the door in lolloped Jessie's two greyhounds, completely un-phased about being in a different country or a new house. They were black like Alfie's and as they came in there was a tidal wave of tail wagging that surged through the lounge. A wag fest. But being greyhounds, within just a couple of minutes they'd all completely exhausted themselves and flopped en masse in front of the log burner, like a panting rug of dogs!

The conversation that lunch time flowed freely between Sam's guests. Sam even amazed himself with the fact that he was enjoying having Jessie Brooks here, in his home. Maybe he enjoyed her being around now because he felt he knew who he was. Now he knew he was Sam Marsh the chieftain of the Lofoten Islands, not Sam Marsh the orphan. For once most of the loose ends in Sam's life seemed to be completely tied up. All except one, that of his Great Grandfather, Herr Krater.

"OY! Have you lot seen the news?" Spike blurted out as everyone chattered, sitting with drinks and nibbles.

"What's that Spike?" asked Svend, "Take your earphones off will you and tell us?"

"Oh yeah, sorry."

"What news?" asked Alfie.

"The news from Austria."

"What news from Austria?" asked Sam suddenly in a panic, Oldemor and Jenny were in Austria, "Where in Austria?"

"Err, dunno, wait a minute."

"Where Spike? Vienna?" Sam was suddenly in a blind panic.

"Naw, naw, err, let me see, Kitzbühel I think, yeah, Kitzbühel. Dunno where it is but it's got to be miles from Vienna!"

Sam breathed a huge sigh of relief. At least it wasn't in Vienna.

Odd reached for the remote and turned the TV on. He selected BBC World News.

"...there is a scene of utter carnage here in Kitzbühel," said a reporter who was stood on a snowy mountainside. The sun was shining but there seemed to be black smoke billowing up behind him, *"the 3S Aerial Tramway has for some reason completely collapsed, I believe, err from speaking to eye witnesses, that the wires that make up the tramway itself have snapped. At the present time this is unconfirmed though. I repeat, this is unconfirmed. Apparently there were many carriages on the sky bridge at the time of the accident and we are told that they crashed straight to the ground, hundreds of metres below. At the moment there are fifty reported casualties, no fatalities, but the Austrian authorities state that they expect this to change. For now, from me, back to the studio."*

Chapter 16

Sunday 1st January 2012, 12.45 pm, high above the Kitzbühel 3S Aerial Tramway, Kitzbühel, Austria. Fly attack!

Simon Lu had been careful not to take his eyes off the Roboflies for a second. He had a really bad gut feeling about them. As he flew along he was constantly looking over one shoulder or another making sure he knew exactly where they all were at all times. But by doing this, his flying was becoming increasingly difficult and he was starting to become dizzier and dizzier. He was feeling terribly air sick. Lu knew that this was what the robot insects were waiting for, for Simon to become confused and then somehow become weakened, then they'd move in for the kill.

As he flew along, for a split second Simon's concentration lapsed and he plummeted like a stone out of the sky towards the heavily laden aerial tramway. Quick as a flash the flies pounced on him like hawks hunting their prey. Thankfully, at the very last second Simon somehow managed to regain control and pull out of the dive just before he hit a carriage. Most of the flies also managed to change direction, but one of them didn't and it smashed straight into the tram car like an out of control scud missile.

The carriage exploded into a ball of flames, breaking its

connection with the tramway and then dropped from the wires towards the ground far below. It dropped like a stone. Anyone in that carriage would have been dead the second the robot hit it. They had no chance.

Knocked right off course by the force of the blast Simon was careering out of control towards another of the carriages.

Smelling blood the remaining flies followed him closely, ready to strike at him. But again at the last minute Simon managed to regain control and changed direction just in time to avoid the carriage. It all happened so fast and the two flies that were closest to him couldn't change course, there wasn't long enough for even their highly attuned robot brains to react.

The Roboflies smashed into the carriage and the explosion seemed to set off a chain reaction along over a dozen more of the aerial compartments. The blasts were immense and threw Simon off course and high into the air. He lost control again and went higher and higher, faster and faster, four hundred miles per hour, five hundred, six, seven, eight, and nine. He went well past the speed of sound (768 miles per hour) and hit a sonic boom that knocked him unconscious as he entered the stratosphere.

Chapter 17

Sunday 1st January 2012, 1pm. Outside the Wiener Musikverein (Vienna Concert Hall), Vienna, Austria.

Jenny James and Freyer Becken were dressed in beautiful expensive outfits which they'd bought on a recent shopping trip to Milan especially for their trip to Vienna. Jenny was dressed in a red, taffeta top with thin shoulder straps all of which sparkled with tiny diamonds in the afternoon sun and tight, black, shimmering cropped leggings whilst Freyer Becken looked every inch the great grandmother of a prince in a purple velvet suit. Each of them had spared no expense on their jewellery either, Freyer Becken preferring gold whilst Jenny had splashed out on a delicate band of platinum for a necklace with a matching bracelet both holding a tiny diamond in the centre of the circle.

They were just coming out of the impressive concert hall known as the Musikverein onto Dumbastraße and were looking for a small cafe to have a spot of lunch before they caught their scheduled three pm private chartered flight back to Oslo.

As they walked away from the steps of the theatre there was a loud explosion behind them and they turned to see huge billows of smoke from the upper areas of the historic building as flames began to lick up into the sky.

People were running out screaming, ball gowns were on fire and gentlemen were flapping their morning jackets wildly trying to extinguish flames.

"Aus! Aus!" A security man was shouting "lassen Sie das Gebäude!"

"He's shouting to everyone to leave the building," said Freyer translating.

"I don't think they need telling." shouted Jenny, who was her normal calm self, "I think they already are!"

"I think we should run, Jenny!" said Freyer, tugging at Jenny's arm.

"Wait!" said Jenny, stopping and turning round, "Did you hear that noise?"

"What noise?"

"The screams."

"Screams? Jenny, everyone's screaming!" said Freyer pulling on Jenny's arm, "Look, I think we should move, it looks like the entire building is about to go up in flames at any moment!"

"No! Wait! Can't you hear it?"

"What?"

"A voice!"

"Look! I can hear lots of voices! Let's go!"

"No it's an English voice, someone is shouting out in English!"

Jenny broke free from Freyer's grasp and ran back through the crowd. The people were thronging and pushing and shoving to get out and away from the flaming building. Freyer struggled to fight against the tide of people but she couldn't, it was too hard. She was being carried along by them, away to safety.

"Jenny!" she called over the din and the panic, "Jenny! Come back! Jenny!"

Freyer reached into her bag and got her mobile phone out but it was no use she couldn't concentrate long enough to use it for the buffeting of the people all around her.

"Jenny!" She called back desperately, but Jenny was nowhere to be seen.

Jenny was a tall, strong girl and she easily twisted and turned her body which enabled her to move against the surging tide of people looking to escape. Everyone looked at her as if she were mad but she kept on going.

"Help me!" the shout was getting louder, "Please, someone help me!"

"Where are you?" called Jenny, as she reached the stragglers at the back of the fleeing revellers.

"Down here!" the voice was louder now, closer.

"Where?"

"Here, under this pillar."

Just in front of Jenny a huge stone pillar had collapsed. Acrid smoke was starting to engulf everything, making breathing really hard. Jenny got to the pillar and grappled her way over a load of rubble.

"Where are you?" she shouted.

"Here," replied the voice, who although closer was getting fainter.

"Where?" Jenny rounded the pillar and then she saw him, he was lying almost completely crushed by the heavy stone.

He was a young man in his early twenties, Jenny guessed, from what she could see of him, he looked big and he had oriental features, she guessed he was of Chinese or Japanese origin. He was wearing a glowing skin tight white suite.

"Quick," he whispered, getting weaker, "come here, help me."

"Wait here, I'll go and get some help," said Jenny coughing and spluttering as the smoke was getting thicker and thicker.

"No!" said the man in a stronger voice, "Don't go!"

"What?"

"It's useless, I'm dying, and you can't stay long, it's too dangerous."

"I'm not going to leave you here," shouted Jenny covering her mouth and nose with a tissue.

"Forget about me, here, come here, I've got something you must take," the man held out his hand, it was tightly closed around something, "two things."

Jenny took his hand and prised his fist open, inside was a computer chip and a USB stick.

"Quick, you haven't long, they'll be here soon then they'll finish me off. Take these, look at them, tell the world about the information that they contain. Tell the world all about a man called Herr Krater before it's too late. It's vital to the future of the world!"

"What?"

"No time to explain, it's really important! Just take them!" argued the man, becoming weaker,

Buzz, buzz. Buzz buzz

"They're here! Go now! Run!" he was using his last few ounces of strength to warn Jenny, "Go!"

Buzz, buzz. Buzz buzz.

Jenny turned back to the man.

"Go!" he shouted desperately.

Jenny got up and started running through the smoke heading for the exits.

Buzz, buzz. Buzz buzz. Buzz, buzz. Buzz buzz. The droning noise was deafeningly loud.

Something landed with a thud in front of Jenny.

"Kick it!" yelled the man, "Kick it! Stun it! Kill it!

Don't let it see your face, do not let it follow you!"

Without further thought Jenny automatically hit out with a powerful karate kick at the object that had landed in the thick smoke in front of her. It fell over stunned. However, only for a second, and then it was back on its feet and moving towards her. She'd never seen anything like it before, it was an insect, a machine insect and it was going to kill her.

Buzz, buzz. Buzz buzz. Buzz, buzz. Buzz buzz.

"What the...?" shrieked Jenny.

The weird robot fly creature was crawling menacingly towards her with its huge bulbous eyes shimmering and glinting in the dim emergency lighting.

"It's eyes, smash 'em!" called the man, "Before it can see you. Do it now!"

Too late! thought Jenny, before kicking out and booting an eye from the creatures metallic skull, avoiding its swipe she shimmied around it, bent down and grabbed a lump of broken stone and, jumping as high as she could she smashed the stone hard into the other eye, sending shards of glimmering metal in flying in all directions.

The now blind robot insect started spinning and whirring on the spot. Round and round in tight circles.

"Run, it's gonna go up in a second!" shouted the man weakly, his strength almost used up.

Jenny grabbed the first eye tucked it under arm like a rugby ball, ducked her head down and ran as fast as she could for the exit.

"Run!"

BANG!!!!!!!!!!!!!!!!!!!!!!!!

The entire area erupted in a ball of flame sending Jenny flying right out onto Dumbastraße, her clothes acting like a parachute and into the arms of a waiting fireman.

Chapter 18

Sunday 1st January 2012, 3.10pm, the Royal Villa, Svolvaer. Text from Jenny to Sam.

Beep, *beep! Beep, beep! Beep, beep!* Sam Marsh's mobile phone buzzed and vibrated gently. Sam picked it up and looked at his messages.

"Anyone we know?" asked Svend curiously.

"Jenny," replied Sam not looking up, still reading, "Oh no!" he blurted out.

"What? What is it Sam?" replied a worried Svend.

"What is it? Has something happened?" asked Odd, jumping to his feet and rushing over to Sam, "I knew I should have gone with them!"

"Err, just wait a minute, let me read it through again," Sam hadn't read the text properly the first time, he needed a few seconds to get it right in his head.

"Sam, Sam! What does she say?" asked Jessie Brooks. For once Jessie was deadly serious, "Is Jenny OK? Tell me she's OK!"

"Err, I think so, wait, I'll read it out to you," said Sam, focussing hard on the small screen of the phone, "she says, Big problem here Sam, explosion in the Vienna Concert Hall, was not accident, weird robots caused it, been given instructions by dying man, got chip and USB stick, both OK, on flight home, see you soon, J."

Whilst everyone was chattering, and whilst the TV was talking to itself, Sam quickly texted Jenny back.

"Not accident? What do you mean? Weird robots? Do you think 'you know who' is involved?"

Within a few seconds, the phone buzzed again as a new text arrived. It was Jenny again.

"Yes, the man told me to tell the world about 'you know who', will look at the chip and stick when home in an hour or so. Meanwhile, look up the name Simon Lu, his name was on the stick. Must have been the dying man. J."

The TV news channel was giving more details out as they got them and everyone was staring at the telly, desperate for more information. Now another reporter was stood outside the smouldering shell of the formerly grand Concert Hall in Vienna.

"If you're just joining us here on the BBC news channel," said the man, "I am stood overlooking the scene of the second catastrophic accident to have struck the small central European country of Austria in the space of just a few hours." He continued with a very serious expression on his face, "Earlier, the 3S Aerial Tramway in the popular ski resort of Kitzbühel was destroyed when what is thought was a freak wind caused a serious mechanical fault. It appears this resulted in several of the tram carriages becoming separated from the cables and crashing to the ground, killing over one hundred and fifty people.

Then, just after about 1 pm, local time, a fierce fire broke out at the Concert Hall here in Vienna, resulting in what you can see behind me," the reporter turned and the camera panned a scene of total destruction.

"As you can see," continued the reporter, "what was once the splendid world famous Vienna Concert Hall is now little more than a smouldering pile of rubble."

Jorunn walked into the room and just caught the end of the news report, "Oh no!" she wailed, "Vienna!

But that's where Jenny and Freyer are!"

66

"Were," said Sam, trying to calm down Jorunn, "it's OK, they're safe, Jorunn, she's just texted me."

"Texted?" Jorunn wasn't convinced, "Are you sure Liten Prinsen?"

"Here, see for yourself, if you don't believe me!" Sam passed his phone to the housekeeper.

Jorunn studied the small screen and then after a long pause returned it to Sam.

"Oh, thank goodness for that," she said before resuming clearing up the plates and glasses from the huge coffee table.

Chapter 19

Sunday 1st January 2012, 3.10pm, The Royal
Suite, Hotel Imperial, Vienna, Misha & Aleksei tidy
up in Vienna.

For over an hour, Herr Krater's two henchmen, Misha and
Aleksei had been tidying up the loose ends caused by
Simon Lu.

Almost as soon as he'd found out that the young British
engineer had stolen one of his precious inventions, Herr Krater
had dispatched his two most trusted servants to follow Lu and
tidy up any fallout from his unexpected departure. As usual their
orders were to use any means at their disposal, threats, lies,
bribes, whatever was needed, to convince the world that what
they actually saw with their own eyes was not, in fact, the truth.

'Tidying up' was an occupational hazard of running a high
tech development organisation such as The Company. Absolute
secrecy was vital but there were times when this information
blackout was compromised. And this compromising was more
often than not because of rogue employees who became nosy,
uncomfortable or scared, or an unfortunate mixture of all three.

Misha Asimov and Aleksei Batkin, like Chigashev and Frolov
were ex KGB agents, but whereas the latter were the brawns, the
former were the brains.

Although they looked like what they really were, gangsters

from the Siberian city of Irkutsk, deep in the Russian hinterland, they were extremely talented organisers and each spoke many different languages. After many years of honing their talents, they could organise or make almost anything happen, they could also make the real reasons things happened, change or disappear.

That's what the two had been doing since they arrived in Vienna and now the men were sat in the comfortable splendour of the Royal Suite at the Hotel Imperial sipping tea with their boss. After a busy few hours their work in the ancient city was now complete.

"So?" said Herr Krater sipping hot Earl Grey tea with lemon from an antique bone china cup.

Herr Krater was a man who liked the very best things in life, the best food, the best restaurants, the best cars, houses, helicopters and when he visited a city where he didn't actually own a property he always stayed in the very best five star hotels. The Hotel Imperial, Vienna, was the best. It provided the billionaire with unbelievably sumptuous surroundings and peace and quiet. Originally created in 1863 as the Vienna residence of the prince of Württemberg and then transformed into a hotel ten years later by him, it was totally palatial. In fact the Royal Suite that Krater was staying in had actually been the residence of the Prince himself. Although Herr Krater detested royalty he certainly liked the splendour that they enjoyed.

"Tidied," said the older and more gnarled looking of the two men, Aleksei Batkin.

Batkin had an ugly weather beaten, pock marked face and a mouth filled with disgusting brown teeth, in fact his nickname was Brown Teeth. The odour was not entirely pleasant either. Batkin was an experienced hand, he had worked for The Company for almost fifteen years whereas his young colleague, Misha, had only been with them for just over two and a half years.

Misha Asimov was almost the exact opposite of Batkin, he was youthful looking, with perfect white skin and sparkling white teeth that almost glistened in the sunlight. In fact he prided himself on his very smart appearance and was secretly repulsed by his, less than attractive, colleague. He'd got the job with The Company because Batkin was a family friend though and had put in a good word for him with Herr Krater.

"And the Aerial Tramway?" asked Herr Krater, eating a delicate cucumber sandwich, which was in white fluffy bread with the crusts removed.

Brown Teeth nodded to Misha to continue.

Misha had a first edition of the evening newspaper and read out loud the front page story.

"...destroyed when a freak wind caused a mechanical fault, resulting in several tram carriages becoming separated from the cables and crashing to the ground."

"Perfect," nodded Herr Krater taking another bite, "and the Musikverein?"

Again Brown Teeth nodded to his young apprentice, who eagerly read again from the crisp paper.

"Just after 1 pm, a fire broke out at the Musikverein. According to the Vienna Fire Department a freak bolt of lightning struck the roof, set alight some ancient rafters and the fire rapidly swept down through the building."

"Very good Gentlemen, and the suit?"

Misha held up a clear polythene bag with a few remnants of charred white cloth inside.

"Good," nodded Krater, who continued, "and what about the body of Simon Lu?"

"On its way back to the Kehlsteinhaus as we speak Sir," grinned Brown Teeth.

"Ah, a job well done, Gentlemen."

Chapter 20

Sunday 1st January 2012, 10.15am (EST). The General Headquarters (GHQ) of The Massachusetts State Police is located in Framingham, Massachusetts, USA.

"So what on Earth is going on? Don't you know what day it is, Green?" hollered a furious Detective Inspector Cliffy Marriot as he burst through the doors of his office of the Massachusetts State Police. His hair was still soaking wet from a very hasty shower.

His long suffering partner Sandra Green had called him an hour earlier and dragged Marriot out of his bed as he was enjoying what he considered was a well deserved lie in. Cliffy's wife and kids had got up early to catch the fast ferry from Hyannis, on the Massachusetts coast, over to visit her folks back home on the island of Nantucket for a few days and Marriot was planning on doing zilch for all the time they were away. Cliffy had even planned his TV viewing itinerary down to the minute for the rest of the holidays.

"Flight 362 from Heathrow to Logan has disappeared, Cliffy," replied Sergeant Green, who had learnt to get straight to the point with Marriot, especially when he was in a bad mood.

"Come again!" Marriot dramatically stopped stock still, before setting off again, "for one second there Green I thought you just said that Flight 362 from Heathrow to Logan had disappeared?" repeated Marriot, sauntering to his desk.

"That's cos I did."

"Ya did?" Marriott's eyes widened.

"Yes Sir."

"Awe!" he grumbled, "I aint awake yet, Green, I need a coffee! Gimme a coffee! Fast!"

"There's one on your desk already Cliffy, black, extra strong, with five sugars, just how you like it," grinned Green.

"Mm. Good work Green, thanks," mumbled Marriot sitting down and slurping the cold coffee, "hey!" He yelled dramatically, "It's freezing cold too! Just how I like it."

After a couple of minutes of staring into space, Marriot gradually came round to the land of the living.

"So," he said looking straight at Green, "tell me this is a sick joke willya, Green. Then I can get back to my pit!"

"Sorry, it's no joke Sir, the early morning flight disappeared. Just gone!"

"Gone?"

"Yep gone!"

"Fill me in on the facts, willya Sandy?"

Green slowly sat down at her desk and got out her seemingly endless notes, "Err, OK. Let's start from the beginning."

"That's an idea."

"First up we got a call from Boston Logan air traffic control about two hours ago."

"And what time did the plane disappear?"

"Well, last contact was 5.20."

"A.M?" snorted Marriot, covering the desk in sticky coffee goo.

"Yes Sir."

"And they didn't inform us until," Marriot looked at his watch, "8.15?"

"7.55am to be precise," argued Green.

"Even so! That's over two and half hours after last contact. Reason for the delay?"

"Don't know Sir."

"Well check it would ya? It could be important."

"Yes Sir."

"Go on, tell me what happened next," continued Marriot, sipping his cold coffee.

Again Green consulted her notes, "Err, last contact was at 5.20. Flight 362, was a British Airways Airbus 380.."

"That's the big one aint it?"

"Sure. Very big. It had a capacity of 555 passengers on board."

"Jeepers!"

"As it came towards America, it was given preliminary permission to come into land at Boston Logon Airport."

"OK," said Marriot, "then what?"

"Nothing Sir."

"Nothing?"

"No Sir, she just didn't land."

"Well, did she crash?"

"Don't think so Sir, there's no evidence of any crash, the coast guard scrambled some sea king helicopters straight away to take a look but there was nothing, no wreckage, nothing."

"Where could she have come down?" asked Marriot, "over land or over sea?"

"At the point of her last broadcast she was over the ocean, radar records confirm it."

"Ah! Radar! So what exactly does clever ole 'radar' tell us?"

"Nothing Sir."

"Naw not again! There's that word again! A detective's nightmare word! *Nothing!*"

"I know I keep using it but radar shows nothing, the flight just disappeared a few seconds after the last radio contact."

"I don't like the sound of this one! Gemme a couple of doughnuts willya! My brain needs food!"

Chapter 21

Sunday 1st January 2012, 6.10pm, the Royal Villa, Svolvaer, Jenny and Freyer return.

Jenny burst through the door of the Royal Villa and ran into the lounge.

"Jenny!" yelled Sam, jumping to his feet.

Jenny looked very much the worse for wear, her expensive red and black outfit was ripped and filthy.

"Good grief! Are you OK?" asked Sam, rushing to hug Jenny.

"Yeah, yeah!" replied Jenny, dodging Sam to stand in front of the stove, "I'm fine."

"Where's Oldemor?" asked Sam looking around.

"Freyer's coming, she's fine Sam, don't worry, look, sit down and listen to me! He's back!"

As Oldemor walked into the room with Odd, who had collected them from the airport, Jenny put some strange looking items on the coffee table in front of everyone.

Along with familiar items like a USB stick and a computer chip, Jenny had brought along some very strange souvenirs from Austria. And the strangest thing about the pieces of shiny metal was that they all looked liked they had once been joined together. The biggest piece was bigger than a large dinner plate, but unlike a dinner plate it wasn't flat, it was domed. Even though it was obviously very badly damaged it was still shimmering and shining in the lights of the lounge. Its outer surface was made up of a mosaic of fragmented pieces of mirror. But it was perfectly smooth.

As Spike curiously stretched out and grabbed the USB and chip, Sam carefully picked up and started examining the more unusual pieces of glistening metal.

"Careful with those Sam," warned Alfie, "we don't know what they could be made of."

"Yes, I think I'd like to get them sent off to Oslo for expert examination," agreed Svend.

"I agree, be careful Sam, you don't know what they could be part of," agreed Odd, "they could be dangerous or contaminated in some way."

"It's alright I know what they're for already," mumbled Sam, examining the bugs' eye carefully, turning it over in his hands, peering and poking.

"You do?" said Freyer, taking a seat on the sofa, "are you sure?"

"Mm, think so," replied Sam, "do you know Jenny?"

"No," said Jenny, getting a Coke from the coffee table, "I just grabbed at this thing, actually I pulled it off this robot machine thing, I didn't know what it was."

"Pulled it off?" said Sam.

"Mm, yeah," Jenny slurped the drink.

Spike had rushed off and returned with some special computer gadgets that he attached to his laptop. He was processing the information contained in the USB and chip with great interest.

"Go on then, tell us!" said Svend, "is it something 'he' made."

"I think so," said Sam.

"Just looks like a broken mirror to me!" mumbled Jessie taking a handful of cheesy puffs, stuffing them in her mouth and munching noisily on them.

"Sam!" said Odd impatiently, "tell us what you think."

"They're eyes!" said Sam, still inspecting the pieces and not even bothering to look up, "Well, I think they are anyway. It's fairly obvious."

"Eyes!" blurted Svend, Odd, Alfie, Freyer and Jessie together in a chorus.

"Yeah, I think so," Sam was engrossed in examining the eye carefully.

"Eyes?" continued Svend, "why do you say that?"

"Look here," Sam was dissecting the eye and pointing, "behind the lenses here, see! There are minute cameras, hardly bigger than a pin head, and there are hundreds, maybe thousands of them here."

"Oh! Is that what *they* are?" asked Freyer.

"Yes, I'm certain of it," said Sam, "I think this is a very sophisticated eye."

"But what on earth would have an eye like this?" asked Freyer.

"A Robo Fly!" Spike hollered.

He'd turned around his laptop and was showing some very complicated plans to everyone.

"A what?" laughed Jessie.

"I'm dead serious Jessie!" snarled Spike, "it's all here, the plans for it, a Robo Fly."

After the revelations of the afternoon, nobody very much felt like having any more New Year celebrations, but everyone was hungry and Jorunn had spent a lot of time and effort making lots of food, so the crowd eagerly tucked into a delicious feast of traditional Norwegian and British vegetarian food. There was veggie Kjøttkaker - delicious Norwegian meatballs in even more delicious gravy, boiled potatoes and tasty sauerkraut cooked with caraway seeds and grovbrød (whole grain bread).

For pudding there was pikekyss, baked meringues, with cloudberry sauce. After the puddings were a mixture of cheeses from Wensleydale, Lancashire and Cheddar and Norwegian cheeses like Jarlsberg and the sweet caramelly Geitost - a brown, fudge like cheese. To finish off were enormous pieces of the New Year cake!

Sam, Spike and Jenny were the first to finish as the dogs waited eagerly outside the door for any leftovers.

"May we leave the table, Oldemor?" Sam asked politely.

"Oh heck! You really are so different now, Sammy Marsh!" chuckled Jessie loudly, "You were never polite like this back at home!"

"We never ate at the table or together!" snorted Jenny under her breath.

"Yes of course you may Sam," replied Freyer, laughing with Jessie, before winking at Sam, "Yes, he's definitely doing very well as the new chieftain of the islands."

"Hey! Can we come up after we finish?" called Alfie, after the disappearing kids, "we want to know what's going on as well with 'you know who'!"

"Sure!" called Sam as they disappeared off into Sam's workshop.

"So the Concert Hall was destroyed by those things?" asked Jenny, finishing her can as she sat on a rocket sofa in Sam's workshop.

"What do you think Spike?" asked Sam.

Spike had studied the plans for the Robo Flies.

"Could they have done it?" asked Jenny.

"Oh yeah, definitely," mumbled Spike, "looking at these plans I'd say they're like controllable thinking missiles! And they're full of explosives, radioactive explosives."

"Thinking missiles? Explosives! Radioactive!" exclaimed Jenny and Sam together, "NO!"

"Well 'you know who' built him!" said Spike pointing to Zebedee who was lying on an old bed in the corner of the workshop sleeping soundly.

Jenny got up quietly and pulled a blanket over the robodiver.

"Jenny!" snorted Spike, "he's a robot!"

"I know but kindness costs nothing," she replied.

"I suppose...," muttered Sam.

"So was that all that was on the USB and the chip?" asked Jenny.

"No way," replied Spike excitedly.

"Go on then, tell us what else there is?" said Sam.

"Plans for other flying machines, look at this one." Spike clicked on the laptop and more plans came up.

"Wow!" said Sam and Jenny together, "what's that?"

"A cloudship," grinned Spike.

"What exactly is a cloudship?" asked Jenny.

"A floating aircraft carrier in the sky. And look at this, this is weird!"

"A spinner," mumbled Sam remembering his dream.

"Yeah!" replied Spike staring at his friend, "how did you know that?"

"I dreamt about them last night," said Sam staring at the computer screen, "I dreamt that they came to finish off what the spider tanks started in the battle for Lofoten."

"You dreamt about them," replied Jenny casting a quick look at Spike.

Spike shrugged, "Weird that is, Sammy Marsh," he mumbled with a slight grin, "could be something to do with 'him'."

"What do you mean?" asked Sam.

"ESP," replied Spike.

"ESP," coughed Jenny, "as in extra sensory perception?"

"Yeah," said a serious Spike.

"Do you believe in ESP?" asked Jenny.

"After the events of the last few months I believe in anything."

"Me too," nodded Sam in agreement.

"But look at this, best of all, look at this."

"What do you mean?" asked Sam, "What is it?"

"Look at it," Spike clicked on his laptop and zoomed in, "neat, eh?"

Jenny and Sam stared blankly at the screen. One side was covered with chemical symbols and equations and the other with photographs of white suits with long capes attached.

"Someone planning on going to a fancy dress party?" laughed Jenny.

"Yeah, yeah!" added Sam, chuckling, "it's like one of those funny party nights, I know, I know, it's the suit from that band, you know the one? ABBA!"

"Yeah, yeah, ha ha! You two can laugh," mumbled Spike, "but you're gonna stop laughing when I tell you what the funny party suit actually does!"

Spike was deadly serious so Jenny and Sam shut up laughing when they noticed that Spike had his serious face on.

"What does it do?" asked Sam.

Spike paused for maximum effect.

"Spike!" yelled Jenny, "come on! Tell us! What does it do?"

"It flies!" replied Spike grinning.

Chapter 22

Sunday 1st January 2012, 6.10pm, Vienna International Airport, Schwechat, Herr Krater departs for his cloudship.

T he gates of the private airfield of the Vienna International Airport, at Schwechat, to the south east of the Austrian capital, swung open as the large black car approached from the direction of the city.

With its blacked out windows and private number plates with just the letters CO1, the brand new Mercedes S Class 65 AMG cruised silently through the open gates without even bothering to slow down before smoothly crossing the airfield in the direction of a private hangar in a discrete corner of the secure complex.

As it sped along, the limousine barely seemed to notice the fuel truck drive past the entrance of the hangar, as it shot into the dark interior of the huge plane garage. Yet the driver of the truck had noticed almost everything about the limo and he carefully noted the details of the vehicle and the precise time of its arrival.

In the depths of the dark hangar the sleek vehicle pulled up right alongside an immense Russian built customised Mil Mi-26 heavy transport helicopter. The jet black 40 metre long heavy duty aircraft sat on the tarmac like an immense grasshopper about to spring high into the cold winter sky. With a flight ceiling of fifty thousand feet this Mil Mi-26 had been specially adapted by The Company's aircraft engineers and could fly more than three times as high as normal.

With over three hundred of these 'beasts of burden' built by Russia since 1981, the actual choice of this aircraft by The Company was purely to avoid being noticed. Although not the most usual freight aircraft you could expect to see at the commercial terminals of an international airport, they weren't exactly unusual either. This helicopter had drawn little attention when it arrived from the east just after lunch time today.

As the chauffeur stepped out of the Mercedes he quickly replaced his smart grey cap on his balding head before shuffling around the spotless car to open the rear door for his important guests. Ducking his head, Herr Krater stepped out of the car and quickly fastened up his long black leather coat as the cheeky icy winter chill sneaked into the hangar. Ignoring the chauffeur, Herr Krater paused for a second as another black Mercedes S Class 65 AMG drew up.

"The driver of the fuel truck?" Herr Krater asked Chigachev, who had hurriedly stepped out from the car and rushed across.

"Gone on sick leave," replied Chigachev smirking, but Krater wasn't amused.

"Did you check his papers first?" asked Krater.

"Fakes," replied Frolov, "Aleksei is checking him out even as we speak. Oh, he's coming now."

Aleksei appeared from inside the third Mercedes and walked up to meet with Krater, Frolov, Chigachev and his partner, Misha Asimov.

"Well?" asked Krater impatiently.

"Mosad," replied Aleksei confidently.

"Are you certain?"

"One hundred percent positive, Sir, his name is...err Henkelman," replied the fair Russian.

"Henkelman?"

"Yes Sir. Y'hoshua Henkelman."

"And where is this Y'hoshua Henkelman headed now?" Krater knew that Aleksei would have hypnotised the Israeli secret service man so he would not remember anything about New Year's day, nothing about who he had been spying on and nothing about who he had seen enter the private aircraft hangar at Vienna International Airport.

"Y'hoshua Henkelman is headed back to his apartment in Vienna in a cab, when he gets there he will be taken straight to his apartment, and when he gets inside he will sleep for forty eight hours before waking up with no recollection of the past week whatsoever."

"Very nice work, Aleksei," said Krater.

As the group walked to the stairs of the large transport helicopter a pilot almost tumbled down the steps and eagerly greeted Herr Krater.

"Herr Krater, welcome, welcome Sir," said Captain Hellmann, grovelling and stretching out a hand to shake Krater's.

But Krater did not shake the pilot's hand. Herr Krater did not shake anyone's hand. Krater didn't like to be touched.

"Are you ready for take-off Hellmann?" He said curtly.

"Yes, sir, ready and cleared as per your instructions, Herr Krater, Sir," replied Helmann pulling back his hand awkwardly.

Within seconds the 'grasshopper's' immense 32 metre long rotor blades started slowly turning. The 'insect' crept slowly forward out of its lair and into the cold alpine evening as its two Lotarev D-136 turboshafts started to deliver just a fraction of their 8,380 kW mega power.

Gradually, the chopper made its way from the hangar and towards the take-off area. Once in position, Hellman gave the power plants plenty of throttle and the 'grasshopper' leapt into the snowy winter's sky and headed towards the mountains.

Chapter 23

Sunday 1st January 2012, 9.10 local (Israel) time.
Institute for Intelligence and Special Operations,
MOSAD, Tel Aviv, Israel.

The chief intelligence gathering officer for the central European branch of the Israeli Institute for Intelligence and Special Operations, or MOSAD, Captain Suzie Elkin was desperately trying to get a hold of one of her operatives in Vienna.

It had been more than three hours since she had spoken with the experienced Y'hoshua Henkelman, the operative she'd stationed at Vienna International Airport one year ago. For MOSAD, Vienna was one of the world's quieter cities, but for Suzie it was her biggy. But even so, things had been really quiet in the Austrian capital over the entire festive season.

Maybe all the villains have to take time off for Christmas? she thought. *Maybe they're all at home spending much needed quality time with their families? I wish I could!*

Of course all that had changed a few hours ago when first the Aerial tramway and then the Vienna Opera House had exploded. The media had initially put the cause of the incidents down to terrible accidents, a terrible double catastrophe they'd called it, a freak or fluke. But Suzie had enough experience to know that this was not right. The media had been got to at the very highest level. The reason they were thinking that the incidents were accidents was because someone had knobbled them! Someone had persuaded them, somehow, that both the incidents were just terrible accidents.

There was no way Suzie believed that! No way! Vienna hadn't been the subject of terrible accidents today, it had been subjected to some sort of terrorist attack. She didn't have a clue who or what had caused all the death and mutilation, but she knew an accident when she saw one and these were no accidents.

As she was sat at her desk pondering things, her faithful assistant, Corporal John Finkell knocked on her door and walked straight into her office.

"Anything from Henkelman yet, John?" she asked.

"Nothing yet Ma'am, but I'm onto it."

"What was his last communication?"

"Err..." Finkell looked down at his notes, "one hour and fifteen minutes ago, he reported heightened activity in a private hangar at Vienna International Airport."

"Which hangar?"

"Err...let me see," Finkell looked down, "the one registered to The Company, Ma'am."

"The Company? Herr Krater?" Captain Suzie Elkin knew a lot about Herr Krater and The Company, most of MOSAD's staff and other security agencies around the world knew a lot about the activities of Herr Krater and The Company, if not about the actual person himself.

What Captain Elkin knew was that Krater was one of the most powerful men on the planet and had been for over sixty years, she also knew that officially he didn't actually exist at all. He'd been killed decades earlier. Officially. She'd heard on the grapevine that it had been Krater who had been responsible for the terrible battle of Lofoten last Autumn, but nobody could confirm this of course.

The Captain also knew that as soon as she heard of any

increased activity around The Company, coupled with any suspicious incidents then there was one man she had to inform, straight away, the National Security Advisor of the United States, Mr Slim Easton.

The National Security Advisor is the chief adviser to the President of the United States on national security issues. In effect, the NSA is the second most powerful person in the world, and without a shadow of a doubt the single most well connected, well informed and most influential person on the planet. Currently the post was held by the tough talking Texan.

"Get me the NSA on the line would you John?"

"Yes Ma'am!" said Finkell scurrying from the office.

Less than twenty seconds later, Elkin's phone on her desk tinkled gently.

She quickly picked up the receiver.

"I have the National Security Advisor on the line Ma'am" said Finkell.

"Slim, how are you?" said Captain Elkin.

"I've been better but it always does me the world of good hearing your dulcet tones Suzie. I guess this isn't a social call," said the NSA getting straight to the point, as was his style. Today he was a worried man and Suzie Elkin was going to add to his headache.

"No Slim, not today, it's The Company, I think they may be behind the incidents in Vienna today."

"Krater?" replied Easton, "you sure?"

"No Slim, not sure, not sure at all, but I've got a hunch and I've got an agent missing who was watching his private hangar at Vienna Airport."

"OK, keep my updated willya?"

"No problem Slim."

"Oh and whilst I'm talking to you Suzie, are you having any problems with your satellites today?"

"As a matter of fact we have got a couple offline," replied

Elkin, "why? Do you think it's connected to The Company's activity?"

"You know me Suzie, I'm a suspicious old beggar, but my hunches are normally right!"

"We'll monitor things closely, Slim."

"Thanks Suzie."

Chapter 24

Oxford Street, London, Sunday 1st January 2012., 6.30 pm GMT, Blitz Kreig, run!

The festive shoppers were out in force on London's busy Oxford Street, in the centre of the British metropolis. By early evening the sales were well and truly in full swing as eager shoppers had descended on London from the four corners of the globe to pick up the bargains that were to be had.

Big Pete Christian was a door man at a top store, a huge muscular thirty two year old West Indian man, he also worked as a bouncer at a top London nightclub. He was six foot five inches tall and weighed over 130 kilograms. Not much scared Pete.

Before the store's doors had opened at ten am this morning it had been Pete who had personally held back the thronging crowd eager to get through the doors and get the best bargains. Now he was overseeing a steady flow in and out of the store. Pete was going on his tea break in less than fifteen minutes and there was a hot cup of tea and a jaffa cake with his name on it in the staff cafeteria, quietly, peacefully, waiting for him.

"Please Sir, can you tell me what time store closes please?" asked a tiny Japanese lady looking up at Pete. Her words dragged him from his daydreams.

"Err...nine pm, madam," replied Pete staring down and checking his watch at the same time.

All of a sudden the woman who had been staring up at Pete glazed over. She was still staring but now her gaze was straight over his right shoulder and up into the sky.

"UFO!" she squealed, frozen to the spot.

"I'm sorry!" Pete couldn't quite believe what he was hearing.

"It UFO!" she pointed.

"I'm sorry madam, but are you alright? Perhaps you should sit down?"

"IT UFO!" The woman was shouting louder now, getting more and more hysterical!

"I am sorry but there aren't any UFO's here! Now if you will move along, please!"

The woman was still staring and but now she was screaming too.

"Space ship! It space ship! UFO! Saucer!"

Pete suddenly noticed that she wasn't the only one, dozens, if not hundreds of people all along Oxford Street were staring into the sky, most of them pointing, and some of them were shouting, "UFO!" too!

As he was staring at the crowds Pete heard a whooshing noise and looked up.

"Whoa!" Without thinking, he dived for cover into the safety of the store as a large flat, flying saucer swooped out of the sky towards the crowds on the busy shopping street. As it swooped, lasers fired from its flat underside, blasting people, cars, buses and buildings to pieces!

It took Pete about half a minute to gather his senses then he cautiously crept back towards the glass door.

The scene that met his eyes was incredible. The entire street was complete and utter carnage. Dozens of saucers were swooping from the sky, droning loudly as they did, firing their lasers at anything and everything.

The noise the craft were making rattled Pete to the very bone, it was a terrible low pitched vibrating noise that made your head hurt.

There were people lying dead and injured everywhere. Cars and buses were upturned and on fire. Buildings all along the street were starting to become engulfed with flames. Car and building alarms were going off all over the street. There was total chaos as people spilled from the buildings only to become the victims of the droning flying saucers.

Pete reached for his phone and dialled 999.

"Hello, emergency services, what service do you require?" asked a voice.

"Err, dunno," replied a confused Pete.

"Sir? Are you still there Sir? I didn't get that."

"Err, yeah, sorry, blooming eck!"

"Sir?"

"Sorry, I'm on Oxford Street."

"Oxford Street, London, Sir?"

"Yeah."

"What's the exact problem Sir?"

"Err," Pete paused, "I dunno quite how to tell you what I can see. Whoah!! Sorry, that was another one..."

How could Pete describe what he was seeing with his own eyes? The operator would never believe him! Who would?

"What is it? Just describe what is in front of you Sir and we'll take it from there," said the operator calmly.

"Err, I think Oxford Street is under attack, Miss."

"Under attack? Terrorist attack?"

"No! Under attack from flying saucers!"

Chapter 25

Austria, Sunday 1st January, 7.35pm (European time), high above the Austrian Alps.

T he Mil Mi-26 Helicopter had climbed steadily higher and higher as it flew across the ancient peaks of the snowy alpine mountain range. Much, much older than the Himalayas, the Alps mountain range is the biggest and highest range in Europe and stretches from Austria and Slovenia in the east; through Italy, Switzerland, Liechtenstein and Germany over to France in the west. Millions of people live within its rugged boundaries but it still maintained thousands of square miles of bleak wilderness.

As the chopper's blades pounded hard and rhythmically, on and on she flew all the time ascending until she had climbed well above even the highest of the clouds that were dropping their snowy flakes on the ski slopes far below.

The chopper levelled out and for another ten minutes it flew onwards over the mountain range until suddenly she stopped moving forward and started just hovering. Then after a patient, carefully timed thirty second wait the pilot spoke into a scrambled radio set.

"Grasshopper to Wheat sheaf, come in Wheat sheaf!"

There was no response for twenty seconds so he tried again.

"Grasshopper to Wheat sheaf, come in Wheat sheaf!"

This time there was a crackling sound coming over the radio.

"Wheat sheaf to Grasshopper, I can confirm that we have you on visual, prepare for the tractor beam to tow you home!"

Hellman quickly took his hands off the flight controls and sat motionless, waiting.

"Grasshopper to Wheat sheaf, it's all yours, bring us home."

Even before Hellman had stopped speaking the controls of the chopper had been seized by something from outside the vehicle and the helicopter was being slowly manoeuvred out of her hovering position. She was pulled higher and higher into the sky. Silently, the engines of the Russian built chopper were switched off remotely, but instead of crashing back down to the earth the machine kept rising higher and higher out towards space itself.

Hellman sat calmly watching the altimeter work its way gradually higher and higher. 60,000 feet, 65,000, 70,000, 75,000. Had the inside of the aircraft not been pressurised the passengers would have been frozen as the temperature outside had dropped well below minus forty degrees centigrade and dropping rapidly.

Finally, as the altimeter reached precisely 80,000 feet the chopper stopped climbing and instead started edging slowly forward.

As Hellman peered out of his windscreen he could just about make out some bright lights about two miles ahead of them. Slowly, as they got closer and closer the lights got brighter until the pilot could clearly make out a flight deck.

"Please fasten seatbelts for landing," said Hellman into his intercom, before he checked his own belt.

But he needn't have worried, everything was under complete control. The large helicopter was dragged slowly and smoothly into the large flight deck of Cloudbase 1 and the huge external doors closed silently behind them. Grasshopper was pulled further and further into the large hangar and then she was placed gently down onto the runway.

Back in the luxurious passenger cabin with its sumptuous furniture Herr Krater unbuckled his seat belt and leapt up before standing impatiently at the exit for his pilot to open the door for him.

"I hope you enjoyed the flight Herr Krater, Sir?" Said Hellman bowing and scraping

"Very smooth Hellman," commended Krater, "you're a credit to your profession."

"Thank you Sir, have a nice day."

"I will," replied Krater coldly, he didn't like creeps.

"Thank you Sir.."

"Hellman! Can you just shut up and open the door, man!" spat Krater as Hellman set to and opened the door and the professor stepped down into the bright lights of the flight deck of his latest pride and joy, his immense cloudbase.

Chapter 26

RAF Coningsby, Lincolnshire, England. Sunday 1st January 2012, 6.40 pm GMT, Scramble!

Four of the Royal Air Forces 56 Squadron's one man Typhoon Euro fighters were about to take off from the long runway at RAF Coningsby. The base is situated in eastern England, just over one hundred miles to the north of London, on the flat fen lands that jut out into the North Sea. Once these four fighters took off a further four would be scrambled and then another four after them. They would fly to the capital in waves and intercept whatever was attacking the shoppers on Oxford Street.

The airfield ground personnel waved the jets into position at the end of the long runway, then air traffic control cleared them for take-off.

Three, two, one! Commanding officer Captain Steve Powell engaged the two Eurojet EJ200 power plants that could take the $50 million Typhoon to Mach 2.0 or 2.1,483mph, within seconds of take-off. Strapped in firmly, Powell felt the immense G force of the take-off thrust him firmly back against his chair as he rocketed down the runway, his after burners kicking in and effortlessly taking off into the dark winter night.

The other three fighters took off within seconds of each other and straight away the aircraft assumed a wing tip flight formation, where they almost shadowed each other in a state of battle readiness, something they had practiced hundreds of times before. But this time they weren't practicing, they were going into battle for real.

Four more of the brand new jet planes quickly taxied out onto the tarmac and prepared to follow Captain Powell and his team into the night sky.

At just under mach two, the war planes would engage the unknown enemy, who was currently wreaking havoc on London's city streets, within five short minutes. All the planes were armed with an impressive array of sidewinder air to air missiles each costing hundreds of thousands of pounds, along with canons that could shoot thousands of rounds of armour piercing bullets each minute. These war planes were well prepared and ready for a big fight. They'd definitely get that from the Spinners.

"What's happening?" asked Phil Blanes, in the second of the Typhoons, over the radio as the small group flew in a wave over the flat Lincolnshire countryside hundreds of feet below them. The team had been scrambled so quickly there hadn't been time even for a flight briefing.

"Your guess is as good as mine Phil," replied Powell honestly, as he levelled out his jet plane and turned south, southwest.

"What was the scramble report, Sir?" Blanes was naturally curious.

"It just said there were unknown enemy aircraft attacking Oxford street!" mused Powell.

"What? Who?"

"Don't know Phil, officially and unofficially"

"Not a clue? Really?"

"Nope, not a clue."

"You're joking aren't you Sir," piped in Jamie Delarge in plane three.

"No, airman, this time this is not a joke, and it is not an exercise, this time it's for real!"

Armed to the teeth with high technology armoury and gadgets the Euro Fighter Typhoon was the latest attack plane developed by a consortium of European aerospace companies and had been developed to replace the aging Tornado Swing Wing fighter.

Whilst the Tornado had a complicated swing wing system, to improve its manoeuvrability, the Euro fighter aircraft has a canard-delta wing configuration, which used two sets of wings, including a set of smaller movable delta wings immediately in front of the main wings. The war plane also included state of the art control systems such as a Speech Recognition Module. But even though the Typhoon was crammed with gadgets it still relied heavily on the skill of its highly trained pilots when it entered a battle zone.

As the twelve brand new jets howled low over farm land, small towns and villages, they didn't know that they would need all the technological advances and the best pilots in the business along with a huge amount of luck if they were to defeat the Spinners with their inhuman skelibot pilots!

Chapter 27

Cloudbase 1, 80,000 feet altitude, off the coast of Lincolnshire, England. Sunday 1st January 2012., 6.43pm.

Herr Krater was sat in the large comfortable commanding officer's seat on the bridge in the island of his pride and joy. Stood at his side was his trusted friend, Admiral Ernst Schneider, a fellow world war two veteran and gnarled warrior.

A large control tower called an 'island' hung beneath the bulk of the base like a stalactite hanging from the roof of a cave deep in the bowels of the Earth. Upon closer inspection the island looked a lot like an upside-down tower block, which had twenty storeys that reached down towards the ground far below.

"How is our plan coming along Ernst?" asked Krater to the smartly uniformed Admiral, who looked over a hundred years old, and extremely bad tempered and grumpy with it.

"Exactly to plan Sir," replied Schneider, who, like Krater, didn't like to waste his time with small talk.

"Exactly how many Spinners were launched?"

"Twelve."

"And they are currently awaiting engagement with the enemy?"

"Aye, Sir," replied the surly Admiral. Even Krater would have liked more conversation but he wouldn't get it from the Admiral.

"What are they doing at the moment?" asked Krater.

"Decimating."

"Decimating Oxford Street?"

"Aye, Sir."

Herr Krater grinned a sickeningly evil smile.

"Have the enemy been scrambled yet?" asked Krater curiously.

"Aye Sir."

"What are they sending?"

"Euro Fighter Typhoons."

Krater rubbed his hands together with glee, "Excellent, that will allow us to make an accurate assessment of the progress of our aircraft and pilots."

"Aye Sir."

"How many Euro fighters have they launched?"

"Twelve."

"A nice balance don't you think?"

Schneider just looked at Herr Krater. He wasn't concerned with balances, not with what the enemy had decided to launch against him, he was only concerned with meeting his operational objective. The total obliteration of the enemy of this battle.

"What is the estimated time of engagement, Admiral?"

Admiral Schneider looked at his watch and then back to Krater, he grinned creepily, "Now."

Chapter 28

Oxford Street, London, England. Sunday 1st January 2012, 6.46 pm (GMT), Low flying unidentified craft.

T he terrifying flying saucers were reaping terrible havoc on Oxford Street. Cars and buses were on fire yet worse, dead and injured bodies were strewn everywhere. Sirens were howling, car alarms beeping and fire alarms ringing. The sound was deafening and it was being added to by the sound of the blasts from the lasers of the craft and the explosions.

The metropolitan police had completely sealed off central London and anyone brave enough or stupid enough to try to make it to the London Underground system had to run the gauntlet of the lethal UFO's who were cruelly picking off their victims like snipers.

The evil saucers were zooming up and down the entire one and a half mile length of the road all the way from Marble Arch to Tottenham Court Road like low flying jet fighters, but without the sound of jet engines, just the incessant droning.

Jam packed with world famous shops, Oxford Street was now less like a shopping dream and more like a war zone nightmare. Most of the famous stores were now towering infernos which the fire service couldn't get to. One unfortunate fire engine, with a team that was brave enough to drive along the carnage of

Oxford Street was struck by a laser beam from a low flying saucer craft and incinerated instantly.

Even the remnants of the once magnificent Christmas lights were hanging sparking and swinging dangerously as the flying machines created their own terrible gusts of wind as they zoomed back and forth.

In his own department store, hiding behind a huge pile of soaking teddy bears, doorman Pete Christian was peering out of the shattered windows getting wetter and wetter by the second as the store sprinkler system tried to put out all the fires that were burning around about him. Pete was talking on his mobile phone.

"Whoah!" cried Pete as he ducked down low to avoid a beam of light that narrowly missed the top of his head.

"What? What was that Pete?" asked the person on the other end of the line. Pete had called the BBC when the incident had started and now he was live on their news channel, broadcasting to a stunned world.

"I'm OK, I'm OK!" sighed Pete, peering over the teddies again, "a blooming laser beam just missed my head by millimetres," he was over exaggerating as normal, "if that! Maybe it was more like nanometres!" Pete didn't have a clue whether the nanometre was an actual measure of length or not, it just sounded more impressive.

"Please take great care, Pete," replied the newsreader sincerely, "do not put yourself in danger at all," the editor of the news programme was screaming in the presenter's ear that if anything happened to Pete whilst he was talking to them on air, the corporation could be sued by his family for a fortune.

"I'm OK. Whehey!" Another blast missed him by more than a metre, "Another one there! And that one was even closer! I tell you, I'm well in the firing line here!" Pete was enjoying his few moments of global stardom!

"When it's safe Pete," continued the newsreader, "please describe to us again what is happening on Oxford Street today."

"Err..." Pete was trying to recollect how this had all started. Even though it was just minutes, it seemed like a lifetime.

"Tell us," interrupted the newsreader, "err, how it all started, where were you exactly when they appeared?"

"Err. I was stood outside the store, I'm the doorman you see. It was only a few minutes before I was due to go on a break, and I was ready for a drink too, I can tell you."

"When did you actually first notice something was wrong Pete?"

"Well I think it was when this Japanese woman started screaming!" Pete chuckled, "I didn't know what the matter was."

"I'm sorry?"

"I didn't know what was up, she was just shouting, I couldn't understand her very well, I don't think she spoke much English."

"Please continue Pete."

"Yeah. Anyway, when I looked up at what she was staring at, I saw em too!"

"The war planes?"

"They weren't no planes!"

"What exactly were, err...are they Pete?" asked the newsreader.

"UFO's!"

"Did you say UFO's?"

"Yeah. Whoah!!" Another laser beam had missed Pete's head by a couple of metres.

"Another close one Pete?" asked the worried newsreader.

"Yeah, real, real close!" Pete lied.

"Are you OK to carry on with us here at the BBC?"

"Yeah, yeah!" There was no way Pete was going to hang up, not now, "I'm alright to carry on."

"Tell us what happened next?"

"They started firing!"

"Firing?"

"Yeah, firing these laser beams from their sides, lethal they are, one blast blows a car up! There are dozens of them too..."

"Cars?"

"Yeah, they're burning all along Oxford Street, they are, and buses too."

"What about the shops, Pete?"

"All on fire!"

"All of them, Pete?"

"Yeah all of them."

"Are there any emergency services there on the scene?"

"Not now," replied Pete, "a fire engine tried to come up the street but one of them alien ships just blasted it and blew it to pieces!"

"The fire engine?"

"Yeah."

"Just to confirm a flying saucer blew up a fire engine? Is that right Pete?"

"Yeah."

"Can you tell us what's happening now, Pete?"

As they were speaking there was a roaring sound. Pete rushed out from behind his pile of soft toys, all the saucer craft seemed distracted all of a sudden.

"Wow!" said Pete.

"Pete, what is it?" asked the newsreader, "tell us what you can see."

"Looks like the cavalry have arrived!"

"Describe what you see can exactly, Pete?

"There are planes here now, war planes, looks like the action's just getting started!"

"RAF planes have arrived?" asked the newsreader.

"Yeah-yeah, they'll show those plate craft a thing or two about flying, won't they?"

Chapter 29

Oxford Street, London, England. Sunday 1st January 2012., 6.46 pm (GMT), the second battle of Britain.

Captain Steve Powell, Phil Blanes, Jamie Delarge and Bobby Mills were approaching their destination from the north via Camden Town, Regents Park and Marylebone at the speed of sound.

When they turned sharply to the west over Hyde Park, they saw their enemy for the first time.

"I have visual," said Blanes into his radio mask, which he had secured firmly over his face.

"What do you see Phil?" asked Captain Powell.

"Weird flying saucer, about five metres in diameter," replied Blanes.

"I have visual too," added Mills in the fourth jet.

"Me too!" said Delarge in number three.

"Why on Earth can't I see anything?" said a worried Powell in the first jet. He was looking all around but he couldn't see a thing.

Just as Powell descended almost down to street level, slowing down to 250 miles per hour he saw one of the UFO's for the first time, then he saw another, and another. But he saw them too late, it was an ambush, two of them were waiting in the open doorways of shops on either side of Oxford Street, hovering just inches above the wreckage strewn ground.

Just as the squadron leader passed them, they pushed out and both of the saucers fired at exactly the same time. Their accuracy was perfect. He had no chance to react, to fire or to even change direction, Powell just saw them out of the corners of his eyes as they blasted him to smithereens. Instantly his fighter plane turned into a fire ball and careered into an upturned red double decker bus, resulting in an almighty explosion.

In the glowing inferno no one saw Captain Powell's ejector seat smash out of the glass canopy of the Typhoon. It blasted him over two hundred metres into the air high above the battle scene and the London skyline.

"The Chief's down!" screamed Blanes, assuming command, "Pull up, pull up, pull up!"

All three of the jet planes did as they were ordered and shot into the sky high above the capital.

"ET at six O'clock!" said Delarge calmly.

"I've got you covered," said Mills, "sidewinders armed and ready."

"Fire!" ordered Blanes.

Mills pressed the big red button on the joystick in the centre of his cockpit and immediately launched an air to air sidewinder missile at the chasing flying saucer.

"Missile away," reported Mills confidently.

The sidewinder shot out from the fighter and in less than one and a half seconds smashed into the side of the space craft. There was an impressive puff of smoke and a vicious ball of fire which enveloped everything within a half mile radius.

"Yes!" The pilots were delighted to have downed one of the enemy.

But as the fire subsided and the smoke slowly cleared, everyone could see more clearly. The saucer craft had not been destroyed at all by the missile, it hadn't been dinted or even scratched! It was still chasing the war planes. Still chasing them!

"UFO not destroyed," reported Mills stunned, "repeat UFO not destroyed."

Two more saucers shot up from ground level and literally appeared smack, bang in front of the terrified pilots. They were being easily outmanoeuvred, and outplayed. They were like sitting ducks waiting to be picked off by the unidentified craft.

The pilots had no choice though, and there was no way these brave men would go down without some kind of fight. They all armed every single one of their missiles, they started firing thousands of rounds of thirty millimetre bullets out of their canons at the enemy! The flying saucers turned to face them head and on and fired their powerful lasers at the three remaining Typhoons.

As the war planes erupted in violent balls of flames the on board computers fired their precious human cargo out high into the night sky, the super reactions of the on board computers giving the pilots a chance of surviving to fight another day.

Chapter 30

The office of the National Security Advisor,
The White House, Washington DC, USA, Sunday
1st January 2012, 2.50 pm (EST).

"What on Earth *are* those things?" said Slim Easton banging his fist down hard on his wooden desk. The desk had been the same one the fortieth president of the United Sates, former actor, Ronald Reagan had used during his eight years in office during the 1980's. Slim Easton wasn't ever a fan of Reagan's politics, he wasn't a fan of politics full stop! He was just a fan of old cowboy films! Slim Easton often thought of himself as an old cowboy!

Across the huge oak desk from Easton sat two men in impressive military uniforms with dozens of medals pinned to their chests. The first, a sailor, Admiral Ben Green, was the head of the US Navy and the other a soldier, General Jerry Brownlaw, was the head of the army of the United States.

"Well I think that's the thing Slim," replied Jerry calmly sipping on a hot, black coffee.

"Whaddaya mean Jerry," said Slim turning his attention away from the huge TV that was stuck on the wall at the far side of his large office in the West Wing of the White House.

"I mean," said Jerry, taking another sip, "I think there's a fair chance that these things, the flying saucers, UFO's, whatever you want to call 'em, are not actually from the Earth."

"You saying we're under attack by ET?" snapped Slim, "cos I spoke with Jane McCoy earlier and she says nothing unusual has been detected heading towards Earth. And I reckon she'd know!"

"Would she? Well she and we didn't see where this little lot came from, did we Slim?" added Ben.

Slim sat back in his chair, "mm," he sighed, "point taken."

Just then the red telephone on Slim Easton's desk rang. Everyone in the office stopped and stared at the phone, *the* phone, the most important phone in the entire world! It was the phone that connected the NSA to the President himself!

Slim coughed to clear his throat, took a deep breath and slowly picked up the phone.

"Sir?" he said quietly.

"Slim, I just saw that TV broadcast from London," said the President who was on holiday in Hawaii with his family.

"Yeah, so did I Sir," replied Easton.

"Well? Who are these idiots, are they aliens? If not where do they come from and what do they want?"

Slim sighed, he really hated not knowing, his job was information and he always made sure that he had his finger on the world's pulse. If anything was going on anywhere in the world, Slim Easton knew about it. Even if you blew your nose too hard, Slim Easton knew about it! But he *didn't* know about this and he was feeling none too good about it.

"Honestly?" replied Slim.

"Always," replied the President.

"Honestly, I don't know who these people, if they indeed are people, are Sir. I don't know where they come from and I don't have a clue what they want," admitted Slim Easton.

"What?" The President couldn't believe what he was hearing. He had known the NSA for five years in total, and not once in those five years had Slim Easton ever told him that he didn't know what was going on. Easton always knew everything.

"I have to be honest Sir, I just don't have a clue!" Slim Easton was being brutally honest.

"OK, OK Slim," the President was a man who liked to work around problems, he could always find a solution, he always said there was a solution for every problem, and he knew the best place to start would be with the world famous intuition of the NSA. The president knew that if Slim didn't actually have rock solid facts, he nearly always had a good idea why something was happening and what or who was causing it. "Tell me what you do know, and start right from the beginning."

"Well, when I was taking my early morning bike ride this morning..."

"On your stationary bike?" The President always ribbed Easton about the fact that he rode for miles and miles each morning but never actually went anywhere! He, the President, liked to go somewhere if he was cycling.

"Yeah, yeah," agreed Slim Easton, who half expected the President to make some kind of comment, even today, "on my bike that goes absolutely nowhere!"

"Glad we cleared that up before anything else!" goaded the President, "go on."

"Well I got an early morning call from Jane McCoy."

"Jane McCoy? The scientist at NASA?"

"Yessir. Anyway, she told me that this morning they'd lost the International Space Centre..."

"What?" The President couldn't quite believe what he was hearing, "Lost?"

"That's what I said, 'lost'!"

"They said they lost the International Space Centre?" repeated the President.

"Yeah. Well, I wanted to confirm with Jane if she meant they'd just lost contact with the space station or they'd actually lost the thing!"

"Right. And what did she say?"

"She said she didn't know."

As they were speaking Slim Easton's intercom buzzed, it was his secretary.

Janet? But she knows that I'm on the phone to the President? thought Slim, *this has got to be really, really important!*

"Chief, can you just hold on a second," said Slim to the President, he knew better than to put the most important man on the planet on hold, especially at a time like this, so he carefully put the receiver down on his desk and pressed the intercom.

"Janet, what is it? I'm on the phone to the President!"

"I know Sir, but there's Professor McCoy from NASA on the line and she says she's got important news. She said it couldn't wait, she was really anxious to speak with you straight away."

"OK Jane, put her through, but she'll have to speak with the President too, I can't keep him waiting. You'll have to put it through as a conference call."

"I'll tell her it's a conference call with you and the President, Sir," said Janet calmly and efficiently.

"Did you get that Sir," said Slim to the President, who was now on speakerphone so the Admiral and the General could hear also.

"I got it Slim, let's go!" said the President, wanting to get to the bottom of things.

"Professor McCoy on the line Sir," said Janet putting the Scottish scientist through.

"Jane, I hear that you've got some news for us?" enquired Slim.

"Yes Sir," replied Jane McCoy, "Hello Mr President, Admiral, General."

"Hi Jane," replied the President.

"Hi Jane," replied Admiral Green and General Brownlaw.

"What've you got for us, Jane," said the President getting straight to the point.

"A number of things, Sir."

"Shoot!" ordered Easton.

"One, the International Space Centre didn't just go out of communications range this morning, it's gone..."

"Gone!" said all four men at the same time.

"Wait," said McCoy interrupting them, "there's a lot more."

"Go on," said Slim Easton.

"Something took it out of orbit this morning."

"Took it out of orbit?" asked Admiral Green, "you mean someone shot it down?"

"No Sir, they took it, we've got a trace on its black box and it's still flying, it's still in the air, it's not exactly in space, it's much lower down in the atmosphere, at about 120 thousand feet altitude."

"OK, so it's still in the air," said the President, "what else?"

"Something or someone is systematically turning off all the satellites around the planet."

"What?" said Easton.

"They're still there, they're just not working, someone is controlling them."

"Someone is controlling our satellites?" repeated the President.

"There's more Sir," interrupted Jane McCoy.

"More?" said the President.

"Yes Sir. Someone is systematically closing down GPS." GPS or the Global Positioning System is a space-based global navigation satellite system that is used by everyone from planes crossing the Atlantic Ocean, cargo ships shipping toys and clothes from China to Europe and London cabbies trying to find their way from A to B in the British capital. Efficiently GPS, as you know, provides the world with precise information about location and time whether it's raining, snowing or the sun is shining. It operates anywhere on or near the Earth when and where there is an unobstructed line of sight to four or more of the global positioning system satellites. The system is operated by the United States government and anyone in the world can use it free of charge. Over the last twenty years almost the entire world has come to rely on it.

"GPS is shutting down?" asked a very worried President.

"Not quite, Sir," corrected Dr McCoy, "GPS *has already* shut down almost completely!"

Chapter 31

The Royal Villa, Svolvaer, Norway, Sunday 1st January 2012, 7.51 pm (local).

They were so engrossed in the news being broadcast constantly across all the news channels that none of the adults at the Royal Villa in Svolvaer even noticed that the children had disappeared.

"What is happening with the world?" mumbled Jessie Brooks as she stuffed her face with more of her favourite cheesy puffs.

The four big lazy dogs were all sleeping soundly in front of the hot stove, totally content with life.

As the television was blaring out the terrible news of the day, Sam, Jenny and Spike had slunk in and grabbed some cans and food. And very soon they too became automatically hooked on watching the television.

As usual the room was toasty warm and the kids joined the adults just sipping drinks and eating nibbles as they watched the amazing pictures of the UFO attack.

The BBC news channel was interviewing an expert in flight, who was giving them the benefit of his years of experience, which when it came to UFO's wasn't very much at all!

"So, Professor Glen," asked the newsreader, "where do you think these UFO's actually originate? Some initial reports have said they're from Mars, which we know can't be true, some say one of the moons of Jupiter or Saturn perhaps, maybe another solar system like Andromeda?"

"The fact is," replied Professor Glen, who had his long straight grey hair tied back in a pony tail, his small, round dark glasses perched on the end of his nose and a thick sandy coloured woolly jumper (which was actually more holes than jumper) completed the picture, "we just aren't sure where they are from, we don't think they come from our own solar system, we have searched it quite extensively."

"Andromeda maybe?"

"Maybe, we have so little knowledge of what's outside our own solar system."

"What about the years and years of reports of UFO sightings?"

"Err..."

"What about the Roswell incident? A saucer crashed there didn't it?"

"Up until now many people have thought that Roswell was a hoax, some testing by the US air force, now it seems aliens do exist, Roswell could have been genuine. For one I always believed in alien life."

"Really?"

"Oh yes, ever since I was kidnapped by them in the 1970's."

"You have been up in an alien craft Professor? Err," the presenter was getting the message in his earpiece loud and clear from his producer telling him to shut the cranky professor up, "well I'm afraid Professor Glen we're going to have to leave it there, tha..."

"I've been up in a couple of dozen actually, they send me emails you know, texts too, when they are in, or rather over town they always call me up."

"Emails? Texts? Call you up? Who?" The newsreader was curious.

"The aliens, ET's, they look like ET you know, and what's

more that actor who played ET, he was really an alien! Steven Spielberg wanted the genuine article so he did his extensive research and through his contacts hired the actor especially..."

Suddenly the camera panned to the second newsreader who quickly introduced some different camera shots of the raid on Oxford Street. The TV station had to get rid of the nutty professor before he said something really crazy.

"So," said Alfie Blom sighing, "well! Everyone seems to think that these saucers were alien craft, and they were flown by that extra terrestrial, what do you call him?"

"ET," replied Odd.

"Yeah, ET, so who could be responsible for those saucer ships then?"

"Great Grandfather," said Sam, matter of factly sipping on his can of Solo, a delicious Norwegian fizzy drink.

"What Sam?" said Freyer, turning to stare at her grandson.

"It's Great Grandfather," said Sam again, he was trying to avoid eye contact with Oldemor because he knew how she felt about his Great Grandfather and he didn't want to upset her.

"But Sam, why would you say that?" said Svend, "Do you have any proof that we don't know about?"

"As a matter of fact we do," said Jenny, "Spike, show them the information you have on your computer."

Spike disappeared to find his laptop, which was still in Sam's workshop. It took him a couple of minutes and then he rushed back in and placed it on the coffee table in the middle of the sofas. Sam quickly grabbed the remote and turned the TV off before he started to explain.

"What is that thing Sam?" asked Alfie squinting at the screen of Spike's laptop.

"That Alfie is a cloudship, an aircraft carrier that flies!" said Jenny.

"A flying aircraft carrier?" said Alfie, blinking in disbelief, "Are you sure?"

"Positive. It's more than twice as big as the US carriers that came to help us in the Battle of Lofoten, Alfie!" added Spike, who was by now an expert on US aircraft carriers, "Which by the way are the biggest warships ever built."

"Hey, just wait a minute, I can't quite believe what I'm seeing or hearing," said the former sailor, Admiral Blom, "now, do I really want to know what launches from these cloudships?"

"Der!" muttered Spike pointing, "These!"

"The flying saucers!" gulped Odd.

"Are you going to call your friend at the White House, Alfie?" asked Freyer.

"Well I think that might be a really good idea." agreed Alfie Blom taking his mobile phone out of his pocket and disappearing into the kitchen, "Heaven knows how they're going to stop 'you know who' this time now he's got indestructible flying saucers and floating aircraft carriers! Slim it's Alfie..."

Chapter 32

Monday 2nd January 2012, 2.52 local time. The Lingga Islands, Sumatra. The birth of a Cloudship.

"Affirmative Herr Krater, Vater, we have just been born," reported the metallic voice of RomyRomy as he stared into the live video link with his father and creator, who was on the other side of the world in Cloudship 2.

"Well done RomyRomy, so my third Cloudship has been born?"

"Affirmative Vater, born and operative, we are climbing to 120 thousand feet and once there we will begin one week of air trials as scheduled."

"Excellent, my son, and what news do you have of Cloudship 4?" Herr Krater was building up a fleet of a dozen of these cloudships, though he knew each one could destroy a continent.

In Herr Krater's evil plans, Cloudship 1 would subdue Europe and Russia, Cloudship 2 America, and Cloudship 3 East Asia. But Krater was a man who liked total power and twelve cloudships would offer him unchallengeable military control over the entire face of planet Earth.

"Cloudship 4 is due to be born in one month, Sir," replied RomyRomy, "with Cloudships 5 and 6 the month after and so on."

"So the rate of construction of the ships is increasing?" asked Krater proudly.

"Affirmative Vater, production is progressing well."

RomyRomy was a robot, the newest generation of artificial intelligence that Herr Krater's scientists at The Company had been developing step by step for over twenty five years. RomyRomy was an RR Class android, RomyRomy was Krater's pride and joy, the most perfect robot he had ever seen and without a shadow of a doubt the future of The Company lay with his android child.

The RR Class androids had a large barrel shaped multifunctional body that was topped with a small round head, on to the front of which these machines could project a face, or any other graphics his mega brain generated including TV pictures, movies or music videos. Like all his family RomyRomy had comically thin legs with feet on the bottom. He had thin arms with hands with fingers that could do exactly what a human hand could do. He could walk like a human, move like a human, talk like a human, he could think like a human but, like a human, he had his own personality, moods, tempers, likes and dislikes. RomyRomy liked the music of the seventies pop star Gary Numan, and his Tubeway Army pop group. He always played his music as he flew, and he was about to play 'Cars' by Numan just as soon as he finished talking to Herr Krater!

This robot was an incredibly complex machine. He was a problem solving android, which learnt like a human as his life progressed. When he was first created or born, he knew very little just like a baby and was dependant on the scientists who had created him. But as his fledgling intellect grew RomyRomy was sent to school. Here he learnt to speak, not just one language but over fifty, including human and computer languages.

The robot child learnt that play was good but fighting was not and so, as he grew up, RomyRomy was able to develop his

117

own unique personality, likes, dislikes and tastes. He also learnt how to be a superb pilot of a cloudship.

As the video link was cut, the electric pop sounds of Gary Numan started blaring out at a deafening volume. The immense bulk of Cloudbase 3 under the command of Admiral RomyRomy was climbing high over the virgin rainforest of the Lingga Islands off the eastern coast of the Riau Islands province on Sumatra Island, Indonesia and west towards the Strait of Malacca. Admiral RomyRomy knew he had to have the vessel at over seventy thousand feet well before crossing the busy shipping lanes to avoid being spotted by any of the sailors who might just be looking into the sky. At the moment secrecy was still crucial. Soon it would not be.

As per his flight plan at the last minute, the Admiral changed his course to south-south east towards the quieter Lombok Strait to avoid the busiest part of the shipping lane.

But as the aircraft carrier changed course and turned, RomyRomy became aware that his Cloudship 3 was being approached by a cargo plane, a slow moving but large Lockheed C-130 Hercules four-engine turboprop freighter.

"Evasive action!" ordered Admiral RomyRomy, to his small crew of humans and androids, who were taking the cloudship on its week of air trials over the Indian Ocean.

RR knew that Cloudship 3 had no choice but to move because the Hercules could not see them. The new technology of the Cloudships made them totally invisible to conventional radar. And, as it was still on its trial period, it was also not yet armed with any guns, missiles or laser weapons, so it could not shoot the plane down to stop the collision.

"The Hercules is approaching quicker than we can

move," replied the Admiral's first officer, who was himself an android and very similar in appearance to RomyRomy, "suggest emergency action immediately, Sir!"

"Affirmative Number One, I concur," RomyRomy paused for a

micro second, assessing all the permutations available to them then he sadly declared, "abandon Cloudship 3!"

Admiral RomyRomy gave the order reluctantly but he knew the impact would cause a massive explosion that could kill everyone on board. Deep down he knew Herr Krater would have sacrificed the crew and just bailed out himself. RR had learnt that this wasn't humane.

At the Admiral's orders, the crew immediately abandoned action stations and instead moved to the emergency life pod which would blast them out of the sinking cloudship and take them home to The Company's Indonesian factory complex hidden deep in the rainforest.

Chapter 33

Monday 2nd January 2012, 2.52 local time. The
Strait of Malacca. Disaster from above.

Portly Captain Stanley Horgan, was a Jewish, Limerick born
Irish merchant seaman and the proud commanding officer
of the mammoth Super Tanker, the Norwegian registered
Lola Pink.

Lola Pink was immense. She was twice as long as the Eiffel
Tower in Paris was tall, indeed she was over 400 metres in length
and today she was fully laden with just a little over 500,000
barrels of Iraqi crude oil on board, headed for the oil greedy
Japanese market. A bright pink colour, she could be seen from
ten miles in either direction, powering her way through the
world's oceans.

At fifty five years old Horgan had been a sailor all his life,
he'd never been married, he was married and completely
devoted to his beloved Lola Pink. As he had no children, he
treated the crew like they were his family. Stanley Horgan didn't
ever bother to take shore leave anymore because his life was the
Lola Pink and he had everything he needed on board. He only
went ashore when his employers in Norway ordered it and then
very reluctantly.

At this hour of the night normally there would just be a

skeleton crew on the bridge of the super tanker, yet as they were travelling through the narrow but incredibly busy shipping lanes of the Strait of Lombok the captain had made sure he had a full complement of his Asian family on the bridge with him. As far as the captain was concerned the more eyes and ears he had on the bridge as they passed through the Strait the better. It was a dangerous place.

The Lombok Strait is a narrow channel of sea which connects the Java Sea to the Indian Ocean and is located between the islands of Bali and Lombok in Indonesia.

Normally, most shipping would use the Strait of Malacca, a narrow 500 mile stretch of water between the Malay Peninsula and the Indonesian island of Sumatra. But because that Strait is so shallow, only 25 metres deep in places, immense super tankers like Lola Pink are too big to use it so they have to go the long way round and use the much deeper Lombok Strait which is over 250 metres deep.

Both these straits lie at a crossroads between east and west, making these stretches of water some of the most important and busiest shipping lanes in the world, and the most dangerous if crews are not on maximum vigilance.

"What in the name of my Aunt Nellie's knickers!" yelled Horgan as the sky above the super tanker was suddenly filled with blinding light.

Everyone rushed to the windows on the port, or to the left hand side of the bridge and peered upwards into the sky. A huge aircraft was right above them, actually dropping right onto them! It was an immense aircraft, much bigger than any plane any of them had ever seen. But it had no wings at all. It looked more like an old fashioned zeppelin airship from the early twentieth century than a plane - what with the basket like apparatus hanging under the main bulk of the ship.

As the spellbound crew stared up at the large airplane which was closing in on them by the second another smaller plane came into view. This one was a conventional propeller driven airplane, it had four engines and was moving much slower than the vast ship. But the strange thing was the small airplane didn't seem to have even seen the larger ship because she was headed right for it! Right on a collision course!

As the crew were engrossed in the drama above their heads a small explosion of light shot out from the underbelly of the huge craft and a rocket like plane shot away from the mother ship with a sonic boom following after a couple of seconds.

"What on Earth?" shouted Horgan, "They're gonna collide!"

Within seconds of the jettison, the Hercules plane must have finally seen the large ship because she suddenly tried to change course! But it was too late! Three thousand feet above the immense, heavily laden Lola Pink, the doomed Hercules cargo plane smashed straight into the side of the cloudship and exploded in a flash of white and orange light. Later, witnesses would declare that they could hear the first explosion ten miles away. But this explosion was nothing compared to what was about to come.

Thinking quickly as any good ship's captain worth his salt would, Captain Horgan ordered an immediate evacuation of his beloved Lola Pink and as every single member of his crew was with him on the bridge at the rear of the immensely long ship they were all able to quickly make their way to safety, jump into the lifeboat and speed away from the doomed super tanker.

Captain Horgan was at the helm of the powerful lifeboat which had been designed to make a quick getaway if needed. A skilful powerboat driver he opened the throttle of the speedboat fully and they shot across the surface of the water, bouncing on the waves as their speed increased.

After the first impact the flaming Hercules dropped from the sky like a fireball. Within seconds a flaming infection spread through the body of the cloudship. She started losing altitude quickly and started on a downward course right for the abandoned Super Tanker!

Cloudship 3 broke Lola Pink's iron spine, smashed her right in two and then ignited the lakes of crude oil that she carried in her huge tanks.

The explosion at that moment was monumental and probably lit up half of south east Asia!

Thankfully for planet Earth, Lola Pink was designed to store her precious cargo in specially sealed individual holds with triple reinforced hulls. The explosion of the cloudship hitting the Lola Pink was massive but it could have been worse for the environment as only a small amount of her huge cargo went up.

The accident couldn't, however, have been much worse for The Company. Now the world could see the evidence before their very eyes of Herr Krater's latest invention, the cloudships! As speeding away from the scene of the accident and into the very hands of the western intelligence agencies were twenty four eye witnesses who were alive and well and more than ready to tell everyone what they had seen crash from the sky onto their beloved Lola Pink!

This day was a dark one for the future of Herr Krater's plans.

Chapter 34

General Headquarters (GHQ) of The
Massachusetts State Police, Framingham,
Massachusetts, USA. Sunday 1st January 2012, 2..52
pm (EST)

Detective Inspector Cliffy Marriot was greedily tucking into his late lunch when an excited Sergeant Sandra Green burst into the police canteen. The normally unflappable Green was bright red in the face and puffing and panting from what seemed like a marathon load of exertion.

If there was one thing Marriot hated it was being disturbed when he was eating. And at the point of Green's dramatic entrance Cliffy was just finishing off his favourite, a third jammy doughnut. When his wife was at home she insisted that he ate salad sandwiches and fresh fruit for his lunch. The Detective Inspector was at least one hundred pounds overweight and whilst Mrs Marriot was away her husband was enjoying a gooey jammy doughnut lunch!

"Chief! Chief!" Sergeant Green could barely speak she was blowing so hard!

"What on Earth is the matter, Green?" barked Marriot, "Can't you see I'm eating doughnuts!"

"But...but..."

"Have aliens landed or something? Is the President coming for tea? What is it?"

"Chief!"

"Breathe! Now! In, hold, out, in, hold, out! There, it's easy when you know how!"

"The NSA's office want to connect you to the NSA in five minutes!" Green was still panting dramatically.

"What? The NSA?"

"Yes!"

"This had better not be a joke! It's not the first of April is it?"

"No."

"Then why are you pulling my leg then? Is it Libowitz? He's a joker! I bet it's him, Libowitz, this is just like him, putting you up to this whilst I'm on my lunch break!"

"Sir! It's not anything to do with Libowitz! He's on vacation in Buffalo with his family. And it's not a joke, it's for real, come on Chief, come now, the NSA's office came through on a scrambled line."

"A scrambled line? I didn't know we had a scrambled line?"

"Well we do, and they came through on it, so come on!"

Reluctantly Detective Inspector Marriot roused himself from his doughnut feast and lumbered after the panicky Sergeant Green.

"This has *got* to be a joke or something?" said Marriot as he entered the office and just as he wedged his fat backside into his seat the phone rang, with the scrambled light flashing.

"Oh!" muttered Marriot, picking up the receiver, "the scrambled line. Hello."

"Detective Chief Inspector Marriot?" said a formal and female voice.

"Who wants to know?" replied the cop.

"The office of the National Security Advisor at the White House in Washington DC, I'm putting you through to the NSA straight away, please hold the line Sir."

There was a ten second pause and then the unmistakable Texan voice of Slim Easton boomed down the line.

"Where ya been Detective Inspector?" He wasn't best pleased with being kept waiting, "I've been kept waiting hours!" exaggerated the tough cowboy.

"Err, sorry Sir, I was out of the office," uttered Marriot.

"Eating doughnuts I expect!"

"Well..."

"Enough of food! OK, whaddaya know about the missing plane Flight 362 from London Heathrow to Boston Logan? I hear you're the investigating officer."

"Err, yes Sir, I am, well not that much to be truthful."

"Have you been out to take a look at the scene of the crime yet?" asked the NSA.

"Yessir, been out there in a chopper this morning."

"And what did you discover Detective?"

"Not a lot Sir. No wreckage at all which is a bit strange."

"Well let me tell you why Cliffy, can I call you Cliffy?"

"Sure! Err...yessir."

"Well Cliffy, I take it you're looking for evidence of a crash?" asked Easton.

"Well, yessir, what else could it be?"

"Theft."

"Theft?" Was the NSA joking, wondered Cliff Marriot.

"Sure, theft with a capital TH!"

"But Sir, I don't understand."

"You will Cliffy, you will, so what I want you to do is to gather all the information you got and get your fat New England butt down here to DC."

"What?"

"Are you deaf now, there'll be a chopper with you in thirty five seconds, and I want you to come and tell us here in Washington everything you know about the disappearance of Flight 362."

Sandra Green was peering out of the station window at an approaching helicopter.

126

"Can I bring my sergeant Sir? She did a lot of the preliminary investigation early this morning, she could be useful." This was true but the real reason Cliff Marriot wanted Sandra Green to go with him in the chopper was that he was scared of going to Washington alone.

"Sure," replied Slim Easton, bring your Aunt Sally or your momma too if they'd help.

"Thank you Sir."

"Seeya shortly!"

As the US Marines Lockheed Martin VH-71 Kestrel helicopter landed on the snow covered lawn of the GHQ of the Massachusetts State Police in Framingham, Massachusetts, Detective Inspector Cliffy Marriot and Sergeant Sandra Green grabbed all the information that they had gathered in the space of the last few hours and ran, well in the case of Cliffy, wobbled, down the stairs and out onto the icy lawn and into the idling dark blue chopper.

Chapter 35

Institute for Intelligence and Special Operations (MOSAD), Tel Aviv, Israel, Sunday 1st January 2012, 10.53pm (local).

For the seventh night in a row Captain Suzie Elkin was working late at the office, she hadn't had a day off for over three months. Suzie had never treated her job as a normal nine to five career and maybe this was why she couldn't find anyone to marry her! When Elkin eventually did get home the only person who would be waiting for her would be her tom cat Oscar!

As the analyst on duty in the centre she was on call and as she was sat pondering what would happen next in Austria and what Herr Krater and The Company were really up to she got a very unexpected telephone call from the Lombok Strait in Asia, from an agent that she'd forgotten even existed. All the top intelligence agencies, MOSAD in Israel, the CIA in America and MI6 in Great Britain, had secret agents stationed all over the world, some doing high profile jobs but most of them just doing ordinary jobs in ordinary places. Most of them never ever even got in touch because their lives were so mundane but they were the eyes and ears of the free world and they played a vital part in keeping everyone safe.

"Hello?" said Elkin, cautiously picking up her own phone, her assistants had gone home hours ago and now only the night shift were in the building.

"Agent 8274645 calling," said an Irish voice. He sounded distant and there was a lot of noise in the background, like the noise of a loud engine working hard.

Quickly, Elkin logged onto the foreign agents section of her computer system and tapped in the number. It quickly came up with Captain Stanley Horgan's details. She discovered he was from a devout Irish Jewish family and was currently commanding officer of the super tanker Lola Pink currently sailing between Iraq and Japan with consignments of crude oil worth billions.

Elkin quickly asked a series of security questions that only Horgan would know the answer to and then accepted it really was her agent.

"Captain Stanley Horgan?" asked Captain Elkin eventually.

"Well, to be sure, I think as God's my witness I still am himself!" replied the Irishman, still retaining his sense of humour. "Although I can tell you me darlin' that I thought for a few seconds back there that I wouldn't be himself much longer and that ole Saint Peter had called me to come up to the pearly gates to meet the good Lord!"

"Do you have news for me?" asked Elkin formally, not having time for Horgan's ramblings.

"Do I have news for you missy?" he chuckled, "Hahaha! Do *I* have news for you, me darlin?"

"Well! Do you?" Captain Elkin wasn't used to being addressed as 'missy', 'darlin', 'lovey', 'sweetheart' or anything else the Irishman would probably call her!

Just as she spoke there was a loud explosion at the other end and Horgan must have dropped his phone.

"Hello! Hello!" Elkin called into the phone, "Captain Horgan, are you alright? Captain Horgan? Are you still there?"

There was a long pause.

"Hello! Captain Horgan are you alright? Are you still there?"

repeated Captain Elkin, she was worried now, what on Earth had just happened?

"Yes, yes, I'm still here lovey, but bejesus! Look at her! Me ship, I mean, she's ruined, completely ruined! Well, she might be still floating but it's her back, it's broken you see and once the spine of a ship breaks she's ruined, she's lost all her strength you see. No strength at all when the spine's broken!"

"The Lola Pink? Are you talking about the Lola Pink, Captain Horgan?"

"Aye darlin, my lovely Lola Pink, me pride and joy for the last few years, she's had her back broken, ruined she is or knackered as we say back in ole Limerick!"

"Captain Horgan what exactly are you trying to tell me? What's happened to the Lola Pink?"

"Something smashed into it, Missy?"

"What kind of something Captain? A missile?" Elkin needed information. *What could break the spine of a super tanker?* Captain Elkin presumed, quite rightly, that they took some sinking.

"No, a massive aircraft me lovely, look I sent you a picture of it, got it on my iPhone just before that little aeroplane smashed into it and blew up. I'm sending a full report within the hour. Err, look, me reception's going fast, it's the rainforest you see, all the trees, too many leaves! It's ruining the signal, it's been lovely talking wid ya, top of the morning! I'll be in touch, Horgan out!"

The jovial Captain Horgan was gone just as quickly as he had arrived. But just as the line went dead a series of amazing photos flashed up on the intelligence

officer's computer, pictures that made Captain Suzie Elkin's heart start beating even faster, pictures of Cloudship 3, with the huge logo of The Company on its side! It was immense!

"Cloudship 3!" she gasped.

Captain Elkin immediately picked up her phone.

"Slim, it's Suzie."

Whilst she was talking Suzie Elkin was forwarding the photos to the email address of the National Security Advisor, *click*, "Look I've just sent you an email. A super tanker called the Lola Pink has just been sunk in the Lombok Strait in Asia, an immensely large aircraft, a cloudship, with The Company logo on it just crashed into it!"

The line at the other end went silent as the NSA opened his email.

Chapter 36

One by one the Spinners attack craft approached the flight deck of Cloudship 1. They lined themselves up in formation to enter the vast indoor runway that had just become visible. Unlike on a conventional aircraft and instead of zooming in under their own steam they each hovered one after another in single file waiting to be pulled safely in by the Cloudship's powerful tractor beams.

Spinner 1 was sucked in and carefully stowed well away from the entrance as the others were pulled home. As soon as it was parked the pilot killed the engines, which were a new generation of sonic propulsion systems that actually used sound waves, droning low pitch sound waves far below the hearing ability of the human ear, to fire the craft along at more than mach 5, or 3807 miles per hour, almost twice as fast as the fastest conventional aircraft, the Lockheed Blackbird, which can fly at 2,194 miles per hour. Unlike conventional jet engines which worked by sucking in air and blasting it out the back under extreme pressure these engines didn't need any air at all to work. So this meant that they could work in space too. The cloudships were powered by the same system, so they could and did fly in space too.

As the sound of the engines wound down the top of the flat saucer was flung open and a bony Skelibot disconnected himself from the ship and climbed out. He leapt off the saucer and landed athletically on his tip toes. "How'd she fly Bone Head!" asked Dick Benz as he plodded up to the fighter.

"Eeee!" replied the pilot, General Speck, angrily, all Skelibots hated Benz and especially Speck. Speck could speak human languages fluently but he didn't often bother troubling himself with an idiot like Dick Benz.

As he passed Benz, Speck threw a can of polish and a cloth at the engineer.

"Give her a polish for me will you Benz!" he called. Benz stood open mouthed, "You speak?!"

"Sure I speak!" Speck stared back with his piercing red eyes, "I just don't speak to you!"

Speck quickly turned his back on Benz and made his way over to the exit door. He was due to debrief Admiral Ernst Schneider and Herr Krater himself, he didn't have time to bother with robot haters like Benz.

"Oh, be like that Speck!" said Benz ditching the cleaning stuff and wandering off to try and find someone else to pass the time of day with.

"I declare the mission to be a resounding success," declared a triumphant Herr Krater who was stood with his arms held triumphantly aloft.

As well as the small team of pilots that had taken part in Operation Oxford Street, over one hundred and fifty more Skelibot pilots were sat in the vast debriefing room learning their new jobs as fighter pilots. World War Three would begin soon and they all knew that even though the people of the world had technology not even a fraction as brilliant as theirs and far inferior flying skills they would be tough opponents. They must not underestimate humanity's response, after all a squadron of junkyard F18's from the US Navy's steam powered battle ships had destroyed the might of Unterwasserwelt's strike force just a couple of months earlier in the Battle for Lofoten! This battle was a sore subject for Herr Krater but a mistake his warriors would not make twice.

"And now I call Squadron Leader General Speck to address you, for my benefit Speck has kindly agreed to speak in human. So, those of you not yet confident in my language, please use your helmet translators. General Speck," Herr Krater proudly beckoned the sinister skeleton robot to take his place at the podium.

Dozens of the Skelibots put ear phones in their metallic ears and waited eagerly for their squadron leader to start addressing them.

"EEEE!" General Speck greeted his colleagues, "Success!" he over-emphasised for the benefit of the humans that didn't understand what he had just said, "I can report today that our first mission was a resounding success! As we suspected, our fantastic spinner craft are infinitely superior to any technology that the humans have available to them."

There was a round of cheering and applause. Speck waited for it to die down before continuing.

"Today we out flew them..."

More cheering.

"Out manoeuvred them..."

The crowd rose to its feet and cheered loudly.

"And we definitely out gunned them!"

The crowd were almost hysterical now. Speck lifted his metal hand and called for calm.

"I can report that the human weapons, when they had the opportunity to fire, which wasn't often..."

Speck chuckled and so did all the rest of the Skelibots.

"Their weapons just bounced off our shields! Soon you will all get the chance to fly our magnificent spinner craft into battle. It will be a battle we will win for each other, for our leader, Herr Krater and The Company, EEE!"

EEE! EEE! EEE! EEE! EEE! roared the crowd.

Within fifteen minutes of the rousing speech, a large solitary, specially adapted passenger spinner craft piloted by General Speck himself took off from Cloudbase 1 and immediately climbed to the very edge of space, it headed west headed for Cloudbase 2.

Herr Krater was going to seek revenge against the mighty Untied States of America! He was determined to humiliate Slim Easton for the embarrassing defeat he inflicted on The Company in the Battle of Lofoten two months earlier. Krater was determined to revenge the defeat.

Chapter 37

The new British Prime Minister, Mrs Paula Hughes, had been enjoying what she considered was a well deserved break with her family at the Prime Ministers official country residence.

Only elected as the new Labour Prime Minister recently, Mrs Hughes suddenly found herself leading Great Britain not only into a new year, a year in which her country was due to host the Olympic games, yet also into the unknown.

And 2012 had started with the worst possible news, London was under attack from what her best advisors told her were aliens! England was under attack from UFO's! It was like a scene from a Hollywood blockbuster!

16th Century Chequers Court where the Prime Minister was currently residing was a large, impressive country house near Ellesborough, just to the south of Aylesbury in Buckinghamshire, in southern England, situated at the foot of the rolling green Chiltern Hills. Although the present house dates from the 16th century, there had been a residence on the site since the 12th century.

For the last four hours or so, the phone lines at the house had

136

been red hot. As had been the front door bell as cabinet members, top civil servants and military advisors had all arrived from their Christmas retreats.

And when she wasn't actually talking to someone on the phone, the Prime Minister, like almost everyone else in the world, had been glued to the 24 hour news channels.

All evening the TV news channels had been showing the scenes from earlier that day in Oxford Street. The cameras had received fantastic pictures almost as soon as the strange flying saucer craft had appeared. At first the TV companies like the people on the ground had thought the flying saucers were some joke or prank. In fact one of the presenters had suggested that they could be the result of some practical jokers setting up some poor soul for a prime time Saturday night TV show.

But within minutes the joviality had disappeared when the UFO's had opened fire with their laser guns. These guns were lethal, blasting laser beams at people, cars, buses, buildings, in fact at just about anything that moved. Very soon the shopper's paradise of Oxford Street didn't resemble Oxford Street any more, instead it resembled the first world war battlefields of the Somme in northern France!

During their reign of terror the TV cameras captured every single movement of the terrible spinning saucer ships, their movements up and down Oxford Street, and the fact that they never ever flew one inch beyond its boundaries of Marble Arch and Tottenham Court Road. The aliens seemed intent just to attack Oxford Street for some reason! And nobody knew why.

Soon there was yet more excitement as RAF war planes arrived. But the world's euphoria and optimism didn't last long. Everyone watched with baited breath as the first wave of four brand new Euro fighter Typhoons zoomed up Oxford Street from the direction of Hyde Park. The first of the war planes shot along the street at a breathtakingly low level ready to strike a lethal blow at the marauding saucer craft, with its three partners following in its wake. But the UFO's were waiting for the unfortunate squadron leader.

It was a cunning ambush and the first plane fell right into the trap they'd laid. Two UFO's were actually waiting in the smashed in shop doorways ready to pounce, which they did as the first of the planes shot along the street. Before the Typhoon could take any kind of evasive action or attack, the saucers blasted it to smithereens with their evil laser weapons.

Badly shocked, the remaining Typhoons tried immediately to take evasive action themselves but they were chased and surrounded by yet more saucers. There seemed to be hundreds of them and they were extremely manoeuvrable, they seemed to be able to run rings around the Typhoons, literally. As with the first one, the Typhoons were completely outclassed by the killer machines and they too were rapidly dispatched, crashing to the ground and causing more buildings to set on fire.

Only when the TV footage was shown over and over again afterwards did the news channels see that all of the pilots in the first four jet planes had actually ejected to safety milliseconds before they erupted in balls of flames.

But the pilots of the eight jet planes that appeared within the next couple of minutes weren't so lucky. They were so quickly dispatched by the aliens that even the high tech brains of the Euro fighters couldn't react quickly enough to eject the men. All eight of the brave RAF pilots perished in what was subsequently called the Battle for Oxford Street.

"So," said the Prime Minister, pacing up and down the conference room, with the hastily convened Emergency Committee, code named Cobra, "who are they?"

She was staring right at her Minister for Defence, Arthur Wilson, and her joint chief of staff, the fearsome General Dame Margo Putterwick.

Wilson, like any good politician, passed the buck immediately to General Putterwick, "Margo? Over to you."

Thankfully, General Putterwick was definitely in the position of head of the British military because she was one of the best military brains that the world had ever seen. The first woman to join the elite commandoes of the Special Air Service or SAS, Putterwick had a reputation for a no nonsense approach where the only option, rightly or wrongly, was attack! A black belt in Karate, the 58 year old mother of five, was a tiny woman, just five feet tall, but the best person to be in charge of Britain's military.

"Prime Minister, they appeared quickly and they disappeared just as quickly," she was stating the obvious.

"Even I can see that Margo!" snapped the Prime Minister, "What else do we know?"

"We don't *know* very much PM," sighed the General, whose short cropped grey hair made her look like a man, yet her pretty face and bright red lipstick quickly dissuaded anyone she was male.

"Go on," said the Prime Minister, "what *do* we know, then?"

"Well, We *do* know they are highly manoeuvrable, they are not powered by conventional propulsion systems, they fire laser beams, but we can also surmise certain things too..."

"I'm listening," the Prime Minister and indeed the rest of the five person emergency committee were all ears.

Emergency Committee COBRA is named after the cabinet room, Cabinet Office Briefing Room, in the secure basement of Whitehall, under Ten Downing Street where the original meetings were held. Now it refers not to a room but a committee. It is a crisis response committee, chaired by the Prime Minister and made up of senior politicians, civil servants and military representatives. Its key responsibility is to organise and coordinate the actions of lots of different and relevant bodies within the British government in response to instances of national or regional crisis, or during events abroad with major implications for the UK. Prior to today the last time it had been summoned had been in the spring of 2010 when then Prime Minister, Gordon Brown, called it to deal with the shutdown of the European air lanes due to ash emission from an Icelandic Volcano.

"That they appear to be relatively short range attack fighters," said General Putterwick.

"What are you trying to say Margo?" asked Arthur Wilson.

"Well," the General was choosing her words carefully so as to be perfectly clear because she didn't like to be misunderstood.

"Margo!" snapped the Prime Minister, "What is it? Tell us!"

"There is a high possibility that there are more of them, lots more of them."

"More?" asked Hughes staring at the Chief of Staff.

"Yes."

"How many more? Fifty? A hundred? Five hundred? A thousand?" The Prime Minister could barely bring herself to think about the consequences for the world.

"I don't know," sighed the General, "but I think we," she glanced over towards the head of the Royal Navy, Admiral Joseph Hartman, who nodded back in support, "are fairly certain that these *short range fighters*," she emphasised the last three words, "are based upon some kind of a carrier."

"A carrier?" asked Prime Minister Hughes, "What do you mean?"

"A carrier, a mother ship, a battle station, the death star, whatever you want to call it, there is, I am almost one hundred percent certain, at least one large ship somewhere very close. Maybe more."

Emergency Committee Cobra was completely silent for at least two minutes, though it seemed like two hours, as what the General had just said was sinking in. It was, finally, the Chancellor of the Exchequer, Bob McDonald who broke the silence.

"This might seem like a really stupid question Margo, but what does this mean exactly?"

The Chief of Military Staff sighed before she answered, "It means, in the best case scenario, Bob, there are lots and lots more of these saucer craft waiting to pounce."

"And the worst case scenario?" asked the Prime Minister.

"There are ships out there with devastating destructive power."

"Heaven help us all!" sighed the PM.

"And" continued Dame Margo, "it appears that they're about to wage war on us!"

The Prime Minister reached for her intercom and buzzed her secretary.

"Yes Ma'am," came a voice over the intercom.

"Get me the President on the line would you Glynis."

Chapter 38

General Headquarters (GHQ) of The Massachusetts State Police, Framingham, Massachusetts, USA. Sunday 1st January 2012., 4.52 pm (EST).

With the departure of Detective Inspector Cliff Marriot and his number two, Sergeant Sandra Green off to the White House, the office was quite deserted when the phone on Marriot's desk started ringing.

After seven rings the answer phone clicked in.

"You've reached the desk of Detective Inspector Cliff Marriot, I'm obviously out so either call me on my cell, if ya know the number, if you don't, tough! Haha! Or leave a message after the tone, thanks! Beep, beep, beeeeeep."

"Cliff it's Leif here, Leif Erickson, look Cliff, oh I really hate speaking to these machines! Isn't there anyone there to pick this call up? Anyone?" Erickson waited a few seconds, "Maybe not. Anyway something real strange happened this morning and to tell you the truth I don't have a clue where I am now...and no Cliff I aint been drinking! I was out in ma boat and then all of a sudden like a jet plane got sorta lifted from the sky by these lights, real bright they were, then my boat got lifted too! Got taken up to this big thing, dunno what you would call it, and there are these strange robots crawling all over it! What?" Leif was being disturbed, "EEE! No I aint gonna give you it, no it's mine, no, no,

don't take it, didn't your mamma teach ya it was rude to snatch?
You stupid pile of nuts and bolts! EEE!"

The line went dead and the message ended.

Chapter 39

Skelibot broadcast to the world, 8.55 GMT.

"We are interrupting your normal programmes to bring you a special broadcast," declared the BBC programme announcer across every single BBC television and radio channel that was broadcast to the world.

The exact same message was being given on every single television and radio across the entire planet.

There was a minute's pause as the Earth held its breath in anticipation. Then a terrifying shiny metal skeleton skull appeared on screen, bright red eyes staring at the camera. Just below the head, on a metal neck, a perfectly tied bow tie and wing collar shirt were visible along with the top of an expensive looking tuxedo.

The Skelibot cleared his throat and prepared to speak.

"Eee! Humans of the Earth, this morning our vastly superior technology disabled your International Space Centre," he paused, "Eee! As I speak we are in the process of disabling your entire satellite communication system, except of course television broadcasts. We have already seized a number of aircraft, and we have grounded all flights due to take off from all airports around your planet."

144

The Skelibot paused to allow the world to digest what he was saying. The emotionless, piercing red eyes never once blinked.

"Eee! This afternoon on Oxford Street, London, we gave an impressive demonstration of our military prowess, destroying a number of your most advanced war planes. This is a *warning*," the Skelibot winked, "we will give just this one warning to the governments of your Earth. From now on no military airplanes should attempt to fly. None whatsoever! If you attempt to fly or worse, take aggressive action against us we will destroy one of your major cities. For your information the first city to be destroyed will be New York. The second will be Moscow, the third London, the fourth will be Beijing and so on."

The Skelibot announcer paused again.

"In due course we will allow you to dismantle your aircraft. We will then arrange for spinner craft to take their places, these spinner craft will happily shuttle humans around your planet and to the stars. We will have control over the skies of the planet and the space of this universe."

He paused again.

"Resistance will not be tolerated but co-operation will be rewarded. You will now be returned to your normal programmes. Thank you and enjoy your evening."

After the broadcast in the Royal Villa in Svolvaer, while the adults were taking in what they had just seen, Sam Marsh jumped to his feet and rushed out of the room.

The rest of the world might be taken in by his tricks, he thought, *but I'm not. They're not aliens, they're Herr Krater's machines!*

Sam had a plan, he remembered his dream and he realised that the only way he could fight his grandfather was with his own technology and he'd do it alone if no one would help him!

Chapter 40

Sam Marsh's workshop, Svolvaer, Lofoten Islands, Sunday 1st January 2012, 10.10pm.

It was a good fifteen minutes before anyone even noticed that Sam was missing, then it was only Spike and Jenny who did. They immediately knew where he would be and what he would be doing.

The pair rushed into Sam's workshop where they discovered him hard at work. The young inventor had set up a series of weird gadgets and machines. There was a specially adapted microwave oven, a Bunsen burner, a series of glass pipes, a mechanical spinning wheel and a makeshift weaving loom that he had borrowed from an old mill back in Yorkshire and had shipped out just a few weeks before Christmas. At the time he didn't really know why he wanted an old loom, but it was going to be broken up as scrap and Sam knew it would come in useful sometime.

Sam was heaving Jorun's old sewing machine from the kitchen and trying to figure out how it worked. It was the one gadget he'd never quite figured out.

"Sam," shrieked Jenny, "isn't that Jorun's sewing machine?"

"Yeah," replied Sam, lifting the machine up onto a table."

"Have you asked her if you can use it?"

"Err, well I did but she was sort of occupied with the telly."

"So she didn't say you could use it?" Jenny was worried.

"I'll put it back before she even notices it's gone."

"Do you even know how to use a sewing machine?" asked Spike gawping at the set up.

"No, but Jenny does," replied Sam smiling at his friend with a pleading look on his face.

"Oh no!" snapped Jenny, "No way, I want no part of this Sam Marsh." replied Jenny.

"Jenny it's vital," pleaded Sam.

"What? Like vital to the survival of the planet?" joked Jenny.

"Yes!" snapped Sam back, he was being deadly serious, "It is vital. Please Jenny, please."

"Oh, alright, what do you want me to sew and I want to make it clear from the start that I am not responsible for any of this if it goes wrong."

Within thirty minutes, Sam had got lots of twine spun from the special plastic mixture he was brewing up with his microwave and Bunsen burner. He used the twine to set up the loom and had woven metres and metres of strange plastic material.

With some of the material, Jenny had used a pattern Spike had downloaded from the internet to cut out some shapes. And then she'd expertly sewn it all together. There was load and loads of material left, easily enough to make two dozen more suits. Flying suits.

"Tada!" announced Jenny, holding three of the suits up.

"What? Is that them?" snuffled Spike laughing, "I can't fit into that! They're tiny!"

And indeed they were, easily no bigger than a costume for a child's doll.

"They expand Derr brain!" gnarled Jenny, pulling a face at Spike.

"They're elastic, Spike!" added Sam enthusiastically, "Now can you get some more made up?"

"Why?" replied Jenny.

"You'll see," grinned Sam.

Thirty minutes later Jenny was exhausted at making endless suits. Sam, who had disappeared into his private, experimental area returned pulling a suit on over his clothes.

"Come on!" he said as he pulled an old motor cycle helmet over his head.

"What are you doing, Sam?" said Jenny.

"What?" mumbled Sam, "I can't hear you from inside the helmet, put yours on and we can talk through the intercom."

Jenny picked up a helmet and put her face inside it, "I said 'What are you doing?"

"Oh, I'm going to find that cloudship that Simon Lu told us about."

"You're doing what?" shouted Jenny.

"I'm going to find the cloudship," repeated Sam, pulling old leather motorbike gloves onto his hands.

"Then what?" asked Jenny

"Dunno," replied Sam honestly, "but I'll figure something out, I always do, now are you two coming?"

Spike was already kitted out and had pulled on his gloves and helmet.

"Ready!" said Spike excitedly.

"Jenny, are you coming?"

"No, I'm not, if you two are dead set on going and I don't like using that word, I think I'd better stay here and tell the others where you've gone."

"Oh come on Jenny," pleaded Sam.

"No leave her alone, Sam," said Spike.

"OK, whatever you want Jenny," agreed Sam reluctantly.

As they walked outside Jenny stopped her friends.

"How will you find it, the cloudship I mean?" she said.

"This," said Sam holding out a piece of the eye of the robot fly.

"A piece of that eye?" asked Jenny.

"Yeah."

"Explain."

"It's their technology and reading Simon Lu's notes I know all of their technology is designed to 'home'."

"To what?" asked Jenny.

"To go home, it'll find its way home, well not a tiny piece like this but a full Robofly or a Robodiver like Zebedee, I had to take out his homing device or he would have just walked out of that door!"

"So?"

"So, if I put it into this device, which is like a Satellite GPS system, it's looking for cloudships, it'll take me to the closest one."

"Bit risky isn't it Sam?" asked Jenny.

"No, it's foolproof," Sam was confident, "and look," Sam pointed to another device that was lying on the side, "I've made two so the others can follow us later, when you tell them where we've gone."

"Oh, OK," sighed Jenny, "Well if I can't talk you two idiots out of this hair brained scheme I better wish you luck."

"Thanks," said Sam, who turned and whistled back into the secret workshop.

"Who are you whistling for?" asked Jenny.

"Wait and see," mumbled Sam.

There was a lot of shuffling noise coming from the workshop and then Zebedee walked out, dressed in a flying suit.

"You're taking Zebedee!" asked Jenny, "I thought he was asleep."

"Wicked!" grinned Spike.

"Reporting for duty Sir!" saluted the tall Robodiver, "Request permission to assemble the attack party!"

"Attack party?" Jenny shook her head.

"Permission granted!" replied Sam.

"Attack party assemble!" shouted Zebedee and one by one

149

twelve more Robodivers appeared out of the workshop and stood to attention. They weren't as shiny as Zebedee and appeared to be made from bits of scrap metal and plastic, but they were definitely fully working Robodivers, Robodivers that Sam Marsh and Zebedee had built! They were each wearing a flying suit.

"Well wicked!" laughed Spike, "We've got ourselves a robot army!"

"Spike, you're not American yet!" scolded Jenny.

"Sorry," mumbled Spike.

"Attack party ready Sir!" reported Zebedee.

"Cheers!" said Sam, "See you later Jen!"

Spike and Sam walked well away from the house and Sam switched his homing device on. He'd fitted a special breathing attachment inside the helmets just in case they had to fly high and before they leapt into the dark cold night he switched his oxygen on.

"Turn your oxygen on Spike," he ordered his friend.

"Roger that, Sam," replied Spike.

"Ready for take-off, Spike."

"Roger that too, Sam!"

"Will you stop talking like that Spike, didn't you hear Jenny, just talk properly!" snapped Sam.

"Oh, alright," accepted Spike.

Spike and Sam waved at Jenny, who waved back and then they counted down.

"Three...two...one...BLAST OFF!"

They all, humans and Robodivers each crouched down low then they took massive leaps. Instead of jumping just a few feet as they would have done normally they were suddenly rocketing into the sky.

One hundred feet, two hundred, three! Five hundred, one thousand, two! Within ten seconds they were at twenty thousand feet.

"Spike, how're you doing?" asked Sam who was an expert flyer, albeit in a rocket chair!

"Fine, weird though innit?"

"Just move your body as you would if you were diving under water," ordered Sam.

When Spike did this he found he could move about easily.

"Are you OK Zebedee?" enquired Sam.

"Affirmative Sir, it's just like swimming, but in the air!" replied the Robodiver who was moving expertly.

After another minute or so Sam spoke again, this time he was serious.

"Come on Spike, Zebedee, team, link arms, we've got to find one of these Cloudbases, and I'm the only one with a homing device."

Spike held on to Sam and the Robodivers linked up as they flew in a south westerly direction towards the southern North.

Chapter 41

The testing of the Cloudship Primary Weapon,

Sunday 1st January 2010, 8.00 pm EST

After seeing the amazing pictures from Captain Suzie Elkin of MOSAD, Slim Easton had a better idea what he was up against. He now knew it wasn't alien technology but an invention of Herr Krater and The Company, some kind of flying aircraft carrier or cloudship.

In the darkness of the winter's night two United States airborne early warning and control (AEWAC) planes were launched from the Andrews Air Facility in Prince George's County, Maryland, just 8 miles east of the nation's capital, Washington, D.C.

The AEWAC's planes have a large metal disc attached to their backs. This disc forms the main part of their airborne radar system. The inside of the aircraft is filled with high tech monitoring equipment and highly trained expert staff. Flying at very high altitude these planes are an early warning system and are the eyes and ears of the US allowing the operators to distinguish between friendly and hostile aircraft hundreds of miles away.

But although the launch of the AEWAC's planes was against the direct orders of the robot people, it was a risk that Slim

Easton thought he had to take. He had to try and find the cloudship.

On board Cloudship 2, Herr Krater was sat on the bridge with Admiral Conrad Schwartz. Schwartz was a young German, only twenty three years old and The Company had recruited him five years earlier direct from high school. He was a genius of a student and had been a German air cadet since he was five years old.

"Admiral we have detected two aircraft taking off from the Andrews air force base," reported a human navigator.

"Identify?" ordered Schwartz.

"Two AEWAC's Sir."

"So they are coming to try and find us," said Herr Krater.

"What are your orders, Sir?" asked Admiral Schwartz, turning to the older man.

"Shoot them down, Admiral."

"With Spinners, Herr Krater?"

"No, not this time, use the primary weapon, test it out and let's see what it can do."

"Aye aye Sir. Number one, arm the primary weapon, destroy the American aircraft."

"Aye aye, Sir," replied the Executive Officer or Number one, who was Schwartz's assistant.

Ten seconds later the primary weapon was ready and the AEWAC's were within target.

"Primary weapon armed and targets within shooting distance, Sir," reported the XO.

"Thank you Number one. Sir, would you like the honour of giving the order?"

"Thank you Admiral, I would like that very much indeed," replied Herr Krater, who smiled and paused for a couple of seconds before speaking again, "Fire!"

The two AEWAC's were flying fifty miles apart and neither had detected any unusual activity on any of their systems until the sudden surge of power coming from over the ocean.

"Eagle Eye One to base," immediately reported the first plane, "We got something."

"Eagle Eye Two to base, we got something too!" reported the second plane.

Two flashes of bright lightning rocketed straight across hundreds of miles of sky striking each of the two surveillance planes at exactly the same moment, instantly obliterating them, and leaving not a single trace that they had ever been in the sky.

Chapter 42

Sam, Spike and the Robodivers board Cloudbase
1. Monday 2nd January 2012, 01.00 am GMT,
High over the North Sea.

"I t must be really close by!" called Sam to Spike over their intercom.

Sam had ensured that their radios were on a special scrambled frequency so they wouldn't be in danger of being discovered.

"Why?" replied Spike who was relishing flying in the Angel suit. It was amazing!

"Because the homing device is going crazy, the reading is nearly off the scale!"

Even with their special forces night vision visors the boys could see absolutely nothing ahead of them apart from miles and miles of empty, freezing cold sky.

"Won't they detect us or something?" muttered Spike suddenly worried.

"No way, I've thought of that, we're too small Spike so I think you'll find we can get on board undetected," Sam was confident and this made Spike feel much better.

"I hope so. Hey!" he yelled "What's that?" Spike was pointing to something dead ahead.

"Looks like we've found the mother ship!" said Sam.

"Mother ship! I like that, sounds like we're in a movie! Nice one Sammy!" chuckled Spike.

They were approaching the cloudship fast.

"Better slow down," said Sam.

"OK, good idea," agreed Spike.

"Slow down everyone!" ordered Sam.

Only when they got very close could they really appreciate the scale and how immensely huge the Cloudbase was.

"Wow!" said Spike, "This sure does dwarf even a Nimitz Class Carrier!"

"Yep," agreed Sam, "it's MASSIVE!"

"Look!" pointed Spike as they closed in, "That looks like the landing deck door and, oh no! It's opening. We've got to get out of here!"

A huge door at the back of the main body of the cloudship slid slowly open and out shot a brightly lit saucer attack craft.

"No!" yelled Sam.

Spike pushed himself off Sam and they shot apart, half of the Robodivers with Spike and half with Sam.

The saucer craft was heading straight for them on a collision course! Only the quick thinking of Spike and the speed that you could fly in the angel suits meant that the evasive action stopped them being smashed out of the sky.

"Good grief that was close! Thanks Spike." Sam gasped as the saucer just missed them.

"Yeah that was too close!" agreed Spike.

"We can't use the front door so we'd better find another way in, eh?" suggested Sam.

"I take it that's the island?" said Spike pointing under the cloudship.

"I suppose."

"Well, that'll be where the bridge is," continued Spike.

"Yeah?"

"Definitely and that's where there's the most security."

"Oh right, I get you," said Sam.

"What about a rubbish chute or something," suggested Spike.

"Well you can go in through a stinking, smelly rubbish chute, but I'm not!" said Sam defiantly.

"OK, keep your knickers on Sam, we can look for somewhere else, it was only a suggestion, where do *you* think we should get aboard that thing, Professor Marsh the ideas man?"

"Err..." Sam was scouring the surface of the cloudship for some place they could get in.

As they flew alongside the ship, the actual size of the massive vessel really struck home, it was immense, like a flying sports stadium, a floating sky city with huge metal walls that were easily forty stories high.

There were port hole windows dotted around the immense hull of the cloudship and at one point, as they were flying slowly along the side of the ship looking for a way in, they stumbled across a staff canteen of sorts.

It was an amazing scene, skeleton robots and humans sat at long tables eating. The people had trays in front of them and they were tucking into plates of food with knives and forks. But the skeleton robots were just sat with their steel fingers stuck in the tables interfacing with the ships systems.

As they were watching the scene in the canteen Sam suddenly spotted something to the side of them which gave him an idea. He tugged at Spike to get his attention which was difficult because he was totally engrossed in watching the canteen scene. He was mesmerised.

"Spike!"

"Err?"

"Spike! Look!"

"Err? What?"

"Look!"

"I am looking!" snorted Spike.

"Not at the skeleton people. Over there!"

157

Spike's gaze followed to where Sam was pointing.

"What are they?"

"Life pods."

"Life pods, what do you mean, something like lifeboats?"

"Yeah, I guess. Anyway look there next to them."

Beside the life pods were little openings, like a chute or tunnel.

"That must be how they board the life pods," said Sam, "do you think you can get one open without setting off any alarms?"

"I'll give it a go," said Spike taking his specially adapted iPhone out of his pocket.

Carefully, Spike felt around the opening until he found what he was looking for.

"Fantastic!" he said.

"What is it?" asked Sam.

"USB port," confirmed Spike.

"USB port? Why would there be a USB port out here on the outside of a cloudship?" Sam was sceptical.

"Derr! To open the door in the event of an emergency I guess! How should I know!" mocked Spike as he connected a short lead to his phone and then connected it the USB port, "Why don't you step into the twenty first century Sam! The trick though is to open it and not set off any alarm bells!"

"Do you think you can do it Spike? We're kind of sticking out like a sore thumb here!"

"We're not but Zebedee and his lot are!" moaned Spike as he tinkered.

"Do you think you can do it Spike?" asked Sam, scanning the horizon. They were safe for the moment, nobody had spotted them.

"Don't think Sammy Boy, I know, I've done it already!"

Spike had unlocked the emergency hatch and a narrow chute had appeared before their eyes.

"You first!" gestured Spike.

"Thanks!" replied Sam climbing carefully into the opening.

"Don't worry Sam," added Spike, "I know where we're going, I've just downloaded a plan of the cloudship too! I've just interfaced it to the rest of the team too!"

"I knew you'd come in useful," muttered Sam as he crawled along the narrow chute, "so I'm the only one who doesn't know and I'm the mission leader! Neat! Come on Zebedee!"

"We will follow Sir," replied the Robodiver.

Chapter 43

The White House is threatened, the President flees in a submarine and Slim Easton assumes control of the US military from Submarine, Monday 2nd January 2010, 10.00 pm EST.

"Brrr, Brrr!" "Brrr, Brrr!" "Brrr, Brrr!" "Brrr, Brrr!" When the special red telephone rang on Slim Easton's desk he naturally assumed it was the President calling from Hawaii to find out what the latest developments were. But he was wrong it wasn't the President at all. It was Admiral Schwartz from Cloudship 2, giving him a stark warning.

"Hello Sir," said Easton, quickly picking up the phone.

"Mr Easton?" It wasn't the President, it was another voice, a voice with a heavy German accent.

"Who is this?" asked Easton.

"I asked the first question, please be kind enough to answer it," Schwartz replied curtly, "Is that Mr Slim Easton, National Security Advisor to the President of the United States of America?"

"Yes and who are you?"

"My name is Admiral Conrad Schwartz."

"Admiral Conrad Schwartz? I don't think I know anyone of that name," replied Easton abruptly.

"You do now Mr Easton. Now stop wasting my time, it is precious, please listen to what I have to say and do not bother even attempting to trace this call it is untraceable."

"I'm listening, tell me who you are and what you want."

"I am the commanding officer of Cloudship 2."

"Cloudship 2?"

"Please do not interrupt Mr Easton!"

"Sorry," Easton was an old hand at communicating with strange people, he knew he had to play it cagey. If this crackpot terrorist was clever enough to be able to infiltrate the White House scrambled telephone system then he was clever enough to be capable of anything.

"As I said Mr Easton, before I was so rudely interrupted, I am the commanding officer of Cloudship 2. Do not worry, you do not yet know what a cloudship is but you will. We are currently flying just off the east coast of the United States. Please do not try to look for us as we are invisible to your pathetic out-dated surveillance systems."

"Sorry," said the NSA.

"You *will* be sorry Mr Easton because as we both know you have already tried to look for us against the express orders you were given."

"I don't know what you mean?" lied Easton, who actually, sadly, had a good idea of what a cloudship was.

"Don't play games with me!" yelled Schwartz, "Didn't your mommy teach you lying was wrong?"

This guy was definitely crazy, thought Slim.

"Sorry," he said again.

"Apology accepted." Schwartz calmed down as quickly as he'd exploded with anger, "As we both know, a short time ago you launched two AEWAC's planes from the Andrews Naval Air Facility."

There was no response from Easton, who had put the call onto speakerphone so everyone in his office could hear it. Sat quietly were Admiral Ben Green, General Jerry Brownlaw, Detective Inspector Cliff Marriot and Sergeant Sandra Green, who was not related to the Admiral.

161

The National Security Advisor was also recording the call and secretly trying to trace it, though so far that had been unsuccessful.

"I take it the silence is an admission of guilt Mr Easton?" chuckled Schwartz.

"What have you done with my planes?" asked the NSA through gritted teeth.

"For your information we have blown your planes out of the sky."

"What? You've killed my men?"

"Shut up Mr Easton! Now please walk to your window."

Easton nervously did as he was asked.

"Can you see the Washington Monument from your window?"

Designed in the 1840's by architect Robert Mills, the Washington Monument was an impressive marble, granite and sandstone obelisk near the west end of the National Mall in Washington, D.C. It was the world's tallest stone structure and the world's tallest obelisk standing over 169 metres high. It was built to commemorate the first U.S. president, General George Washington and could be seen from almost every part of the country's capital, including Slim Easton's office in the West Wing of the White House at 1600 Pennsylvania Avenue.

"I see it, yeah," said Easton warily, "why?"

"Why? I'll tell you why? Count down from ten please Mr Easton."

"What?"

"Just do it!" yelled Schwartz angrily.

"Ten, nine, eight, seven, six, five..." Easton paused.

"Count down!" exploded the Admiral.

"...four, three, two, one."

"Now you see it, now you don't. Zero!"

In a flash of blinding light the entire Washington city scape seemed to glow white hot, and then as quickly as it had appeared the light dimmed once again, leaving everyone blinking their eyes in order to see after the blinding flash.

"Can you still see the Washington Monument from your vantage point Mr Easton?" asked Admiral Schwartz.

Slim Easton along with his four colleagues blinked and blinked until slowly their vision returned.

"Well, can you?" asked the Admiral impatiently.

"No!" yelled the National Security Advisor.

The Washington Monument was gone, completely gone, destroyed without a trace, "What the..."

"Now listen to me," interrupted Schwartz, "and listen good Mr National Security Advisor, you pulled a dirty trick on us tonight while we were giving the world the benefit of the doubt. You will now evacuate the White House because in exactly 30 minutes, no," the madman paused, "now it's just 29 minutes and 55 seconds, we will also destroy the very building that you are now stood in. Good bye!" The phone went dead.

There was no way Slim Easton could take any more risks, whoever he was dealing with here had vast military superiority to the USA, something that hadn't been the case for almost a century. The NSA had no choice but to do as requested, evacuate the White House, move his command to somewhere else, some place safe.

"Come on everyone let's get out of here." said the NSA before banging the intercom button on his desk, "Evacuate the White House, repeat evacuate the White House, code red, this is not a drill, repeat, this is not a drill!" Then taking his cell phone out of his pocket and using the speed dial, he made a call, "Mr President, code red, evacuation of the White House, do not contact me on the land lines, I'll call you in twenty minutes, now you need to get over to Pearl Harbour straight away, you and your family. Don't fly! Repeat, do not fly! The skies are not safe! When you get to Pearl, board the USS Annapolis, she's waiting for you, I know, I know, you don't like submarines but I'm afraid needs must, the air is really not safe and we've just been attacked, yes, yes. What? The Washington Monument that's what, and they say it's going to be the White House next, yes, yes, you heard me right, the White House. No, this is not a joke. Sorry, I've got to go Sir, we're evacuating. We've only got just over twenty five minutes to do it! Call you later. And go straight to Pearl!"

"Just one minute," Easton said to the group as he made another call, "Captain, we need a half dozen patriot batteries at the White House, yes you heard right, the White House, within five minutes!"

The MIM-104 Patriot surface-to-air missile (SAM) system has been used by armies all over the world for over twenty five years as a nation's main defence against attack from the air, as a defence against intercontinental ballistic missiles, rogue fighters or hopefully now enemy cloudships. They might still use radar systems that Herr Krater's air force could block but if they did get a sniff of the enemy the Patriots would shoot them out of the sky.

Waiting for the NSA were the Admiral and General and the two police officers from Massachusetts who were seriously wondering what they had got themselves caught up in!

As they were about to leave the office Detective Inspector Marriot got a call on his cell phone. When he answered it was his voice mail, his cell phone signal must have been blocked all the time he'd been in the White House, but now the systems were being changed, and the building being evacuated, it had automatically connected.

As they walked along the recording started playing.

"Cliff it's Leif here, Leif Erickson here, look Cliff, oh I hate speaking to these machines! Isn't there anyone there to pick this call up? Please!"

There was a pause, Marriot was walking through the passageways of the White House following Slim Easton and his entourage and out to large unmarked, blacked out van.

"Who is it Sir?" asked Sergeant Green.

"Shh!" replied Marriot, "It's Leif."

"Leif? Leif Erickson ? What does he want?"

"Don't know, it's voice mail, but he wouldn't ring if it wasn't serious, not Leif. He doesn't like phones."

"Err, excuse me, and this isn't serious?" replied Green.

"Shh!" said Marriot, Leif had started talking again.

"Maybe not," continued the recording, "anyway something real strange happened this morning and to tell you the truth I don't have a clue where I am now, and no Cliff I aint been drinking! I was out in ma boat and then all of a sudden like a jet plane got sorta lifted from the sky by these lights, real bright they were, then my boat got lifted too! Got taken up to this big thing, dunno what you would call it, and there are these..." the line suddenly went dead.

Marriot stopped stock still, making at least half a dozen people bang into him, the NSA was striding out ahead.

"Mr Easton Sir!" called Marriot after the NSA.

Easton looked around, "Yes, what is it Marriot can't you see I'm kinda busy at the moment?"

"I know Sir, but you're really gonna want to listen to this, it's maybe the best lead we got on those cloud folk!"

Slim Easton took the phone from Marriot and continued walking until he got into the van. After a couple of minutes he looked back at Marriot and Green and smiled.

"Nice work Officer, very nice work, I think we might just be able to get a trace on that flying ship when we get over to USS Springfield, with a bit of luck we can trace Leif's phone, very nice!" For the first time that day Slim Easton had reason for hope. All was not yet lost, the war wasn't over yet, the fat lady hadn't sung! He'd beaten Krater once, he could do it again!

Chapter 44

The MJK are summonsed, Monday 2nd January 2012, 03.15 (local) Ramsund Special Forces Base, Northern Norway.

The MJK or Marinejegerkommandoen to give them their full title are the Norwegian maritime special forces unit, similar to the US Navy SEALs and the British Special Boat Squadron or SBS. One of their two major bases was at Ramsund, a naval base 85 kilometres due east of Svolvaer, Lofoten. They are highly trained Commandoes, the best of the best whose services are greatly in demand around the world. They specialise in small scale quick deployments which generally end up with a lot of things being blown up and a lot of damage being done with minimum damage to themselves. They also specialise in daring rescue missions.

Just one minute earlier Alfie Blom, a former Norwegian naval admiral himself, had told the MJK chief Admiral Stig Berg that Sam Marsh, the Chieftain of Lofoten and his friend Spike Williams were in grave danger and that they would need the help of Stig and his men if they were to escape from the danger they had got themselves into.

Although woken from a deep sleep the 64 year old leader of the force was instantly awake and taking in every detail of the situation. Within two minutes Berg was in the shower waking himself up properly, then he dressed and ran downstairs to the kitchen where the kettle was duly switched on. Admiral Stig took a couple of minutes to sip a quick cup of tea and snack on a high energy biscuit and some fruit. Being on a special forces mission meant he didn't know when or where he would get his next meal, and food means energy, which could be the difference between life and death, his life or death.

Peering out of the triple glazed window, Stig could see that outside his cosy wooden house, which was situated on the base itself, it was snowing heavily. Quickly, he laced up his high black boots and pulled on his Navy issue puffa coat before grabbing his hat and pulling it over his closely cropped hair.

Quietly, so as not to wake his wife Kristen, Stig closed the front door behind him, before sprinting the four hundred metres between his house and the command centre. Normally he expected to make the distance in about one minute ten seconds, actually just before the first snow fall of the winter he'd made it in a personal best of one minute seven point five seconds but in the snow he knew he'd be slower, a lot slower.

"Phew!" sighed Stig as he shot into the command centre and slammed the door shut behind him, bringing in a flurry of large snowflakes with him. He was panting hard.

"Well," said Captain Morten Rudd, Berg's number two at the Ramsund MJK base, "what time did you manage tonight chief?" He had a big grin on his face, but he knew that Berg was not in competition with anyone but himself, that was a major part of being a successful MJK soldier, always trying to improve oneself.

"One minute and..." Berg was staring down at his blackened, high impact special forces watch which could tell you the time on all five continents at the same time, be effective at one thousand metres below the sea and resist a direct thermo nuclear impact. These watches were indestructible. "Twenty two seconds!"

"So by my reckoning that's three seconds quicker than on New Year's Eve?"

"Yeah I think so Mort!" grinned Berg, "Not bad for an old sailor."

"Not bad! OK," said Captain Rudd getting straight down to business, "I've got a team of ten men ready, they're having a light breakfast of porridge and fruit as we speak. What do we know?"

"Well, as I told you before I left home, I've just spoken with Alfie Blom at Svolvaer and it seems that today Sam Marsh and his friends came into possession of some information about his Great Grandfather's latest attempt to rule the world."

"Oh no! Not Herr Krater again?"

"The very same."

"So what's the old fella up to now boss?"

"Looks like he's been developing a number of projects which sit side by side some master plan, number one is a special flying suit.."

"A flying suit?" asked Morten.

"You heard me right Mort. Number two, a gigantic flying aircraft carrier called a cloudship..."

"A cloudship?"

"And various flying craft and robots using a new propulsion system."

"OK," said Morten, "so what has young Sam done with that information, as if I can't guess!"

"Well, it appears that our friend the Viking King has used Herr Krater's formula to develop his very own flying suits and he and Spike Williams have gone off in these suits to find a cloudship. Oh, yeah, he may have taken some Robodivers with him too."

"Some? I thought there was just Zebedee?"

"So did I!" replied Admiral Stig, "It appears our young inventor friend has built some of his own Robodivers. Apparently he's got himself a small army!"

"An Army? Wow! That's typical of Sam. So what does he intend to do when he finds a cloudship?"

"Your guess is as good as mine," replied Admiral Berg.

"So our mission is?" piped up Rudd.

"We get in touch with Sam..."

"How?"

"We know what radio frequency he's using, and he's left us a homing device which will allow us to find the cloudship he's gone to find."

"OK, well at least that's something, then what?"

"We all get kitted out in these special suits..."

"How many are they?" Captain Rudd said unsurely.

"There will be thirteen ready when we get over to Svolvaer," replied Stig Berg.

"Thirteen? There are only twelve of us?"

"Alfie Blom's coming too."

"Old Alfie?"

"Less of the old, show some respect!" snapped the Admiral.

"Sorry chief, then what?"

"We get kitted out, learn to fly like, err, yesterday, and get ourselves up and onto that there cloudship, find Sam and Spike, take control of the carrier, find all the other ones and do a spot of blowing up!"

"You think there's more than one?" asked Rudd.

"Knowing Herr Krater I would say there is probably a whole fleet of them up there about to wage war on the world, but my guess is that he's starting with the USA, with the aim of exacting some revenge for last autumn and then taking over the world!"

"He aims high, old Herr Krater!" laughed Captain Rudd. "He sure does Morten my friend, he sure does, but he aint counting on us crazy vikings flying up and blowing up a few of his pride and joys and ruining the party!"

"We're good at ruining the parties of crazy guys who are hell bent on world domination," added Rudd.

"It's what we do best," agreed Admiral Berg, "now where are

169

all our crazy party ruining pyromaniacs? We got some trouble to stir up some place high in the sky!"

As he was walking into the briefing room Berg took his mobile out of his pocket and dialled a scrambled number.

"Slim, Stig here...really, the White House? Really, OK, OK I understand. Herr Krater and The Company for sure. Well we have a lead...yeah Sam Marsh and his friends...gone to something called a cloudship...really? You know about these? OK, OK I understand. Yes. We're going to follow Sam up to this cloudship thing, yes, yes...we shouldn't blow it up... aw, but that's what we do best...OK, we'll take control of it and come to the States in it... keep in touch...good luck!"

Chapter 45

Sam and Spike are on board, Cloudship 1.

"When will this tunnel end?" moaned Spike in nothing more than a whisper.

"You tell me, you've got the map!" snapped Sam, who was sick and tired of Spike's moaning, he should have come just with the Robodivers, they never moan. He would have done but Spike had already proved himself useful getting them into the cloudship.

"Oh yeah," Spike looked at his iPhone and after a few minutes spoke again, "I forgot about that. We should come to a kinda T junction thing in about five metres or so, err...we need to take the left, that takes us to the engine room, from there we've got to make for the auxiliary control room."

"What?" whispered Sam, "so we're not headed for the bridge, Spike? I thought that was the plan?"

"What with all the security that will be up there?" snapped Spike, "start thinking Sam!"

"Don't you think there'll be security at the auxiliary control room too?"

"It's the middle of the night Sam, so my guess is no, hopefully, well not a lot." Spike crossed his fingers and his toes, he knew they needed a lot of luck if they were going to stop Herr Krater this time and so did Sam, "Keep everything crossed."

At the T-junction they swapped places and Spike led the way. The boys thought it was sensible because he had the map.

After a few metres, just as Spike had said, they came to a full stop. A metal grill was blocking their path.

Spike turned to Sam, and mouthed, "It's the auxiliary control room."

Not daring to speak Sam mouthed back "OK, is there anyone in there? Have a look."

Spike peered through the grill, it was hard to be sure but he was fairly certain that the room was empty, then out of the corner of his eye he saw movement.

He turned to Sam and gestured, "Somebody's in there!"

"Person or robot?" replied Sam mutely, not daring to make a single sound.

Spike peered and peered, eventually the source of the movement came back into view. It was a robot, it was human in shape but not as refined as, say Zebedee,

the Robodiver. Spike guessed that from the look of the robot it was some kind of basic maintenance or cleaning droid.

"Robot, I think it's a cleaner or something." He mouthed.

"Here, take this," mouthed Sam passing Spike something that looked like a walkie talkie.

"What is it?"

"Point it at the droid when you get a good look at him and press the red button, but make sure you keep the button pressed. Firmly!"

Spike took the gadget and waited. He waited and waited but gradually he could see that the cleaner was working its way methodically around the room, cleaning all the surfaces and the floors as it went. It was making a really good job of it too.

It's coming, it's coming, thought Spike pointing the gadget, *bit more, a bit more, just wait for the right moment, wait!*

Then, suddenly, the cleaning droid was right in front of him cleaning the grill that he was hiding behind.

Oh no! he thought, *It's going to see me and shout for help!*

"Press!" whispered Sam and Spike pressed the button and kept it firmly pressed. The droid's eyes shot wide open and its arms fell down by its side as it was stunned.

"Quick," whispered Sam, "get out and catch it, it's going to fall down and that'll make a lot of noise!"

Spike pressed a couple of keys on his iPhone and the grill shot open. He leapt out of the chute and somehow managed to catch the robot that was swaying about drunkenly.

"Give us a hand!" he called back to Sam, "It's really heavy!"

Sam and Zebedee were already out of the chute and stood beside him. Zebedee caught the droid and another Robodiver helped him.

"Here, lay it out over here," said Sam.

The Robodivers carefully laid the robot on the ground.

"How long will it be like that?" asked Spike, "Stunned I mean."

"Forever," said Sam stepping over the droid.

"It's dead?" gasped Spike, "I've killed it!"

"No you haven't, it's not dead Spike, it's a robot, it's permanently off line," replied Sam matter of factly, "until we bring it back on line!" The was a cold harshness in his friend's manner that Spike hadn't seen before.

Sam was inspecting the control panels when suddenly he heard a voice over his helmet radio.

"Sam, Spike come in this is Stig, do you read me?"

"Stig? Where are you?" replied a stunned Sam.

"We're following you over to the cloudship on three of your rocket sofas," replied the Commando.

"You're flying on the rocket sofas?" asked Sam. Sam Marsh and the MJK boys had used Sam's specially built rocket sofas on their last mission.

"Yes, why? We're making great progress! Flying really fast! I love these things!"

"You can't come near the cloudship on the rocket sofa's you'll be like sitting ducks, they'll blow you out of the sky!"

"What? I don't understand."

"Their sensors, they'll be on the lookout for anything that big flying near them, they'll think you're an attack aircraft! They'll shoot you down! And believe me they won't miss!"

"Err, well we're wearing angel suits too," replied Stig.

"You made up some more suits?" asked Sam

"Jenny did."

"And you're all wearing them?"

"Yes, why?"

"Ditch the sofas!" ordered Sam, "Ditch them right now! Fly on just using the angel suits!"

"OK, we'll get ourselves sorted and then ditch the sofas," replied Stig calmly.

"No!" said Sam firmly, "Don't wait! There's no time, Ditch the sofas now! It's too risky! You've got to do it straight away!"

"OK, copy that!" said Stig.

Sam and Spike could hear Stig giving the orders and then they could hear all the commandoes flying by themselves for the first time without the aid of a machine.

"Stig!" called Sam into the radio, "Are you alright Stig?"

"More than alright Sam!" replied a euphoric Admiral Berg, "These angel suits are fantastic, it's brilliant!"

After a couple of minutes of hooting, laughing and yelling, the commandoes went quiet, they had all just seen the cloudship in the distance.

"Sam, we see the cloudship," reported Stig, as he flew closer and closer.

Now the men adopted a more serious tone, now they were professional once again.

"OK, Stig we'll talk you in, we've left a life pod portal unlocked," replied Sam, "come towards the landing deck but fly to the left, the port side of the landing deck. Come alongside and go about halfway along, you'll eventually see a series of brightly lit port holes, try and avoid them, it's the canteen and there will be crew eating in there, don't look inside, Spike did and he couldn't believe what he saw!"

"OK, we won't look."

Sam knew they would.

"Just after the canteen," continued Sam, "there's a life pod and next to it is a portal, it's unlocked and Spike has just opened it. Come in to the cloudship there and we'll talk you in. We're in the auxiliary control room."

"OK, got all that, did you get all that Morten?"

"Roger that chief," replied Morten Rudd.

"What about you Alfie?" asked Stig.

"Alfie's here?" asked a stunned Sam.

"I'm here Sam," replied Alfie Blom, "Nothing on Earth was going to stop me flying in one of these suits, I can tell you!"

Chapter 46

USS Springfield (SSN-761), the new US Headquarters.

The NSA and all his team, along with the still mystified detectives Cliff Marriot and Sandra Green, had left the White House in a convoy of blacked out, armoured vans and headed the couple of miles towards the Potomac River. The two police officers didn't have a clue where they were going or why, but everyone else seemed to know.

Once at the river they had boarded a series of speed boats which all zoomed off down the Potomac towards the Washington Navy Yard. The Washington Navy Yard is the oldest US Navy shore base and currently served as a ceremonial and administrative centre for the entire Navy.

It was not normally a submarine base but tonight waiting in a dark, covered dock was the shadowy Los Angeles-class submarine, USS Springfield (SSN-761). At over 110 m long and a weight of over 6,000 tons, the Springfield and the other 45 LA Class subs had been a crucial part of the defence of the free world for over twenty years. Powered by a S6G nuclear reactor these masters of stealth had the ability to remain completely undetected for months at a time in the depths of the ocean. It was this stealth that Slim Easton was counting on now if the world were to overcome the threat from these new terrorists, which he now knew to be Herr Krater and The Company. After the call from Leif Erickson he knew exactly how he could find them, though he was aware that he would only have one shot at actually pinpointing their position.

"Stig can you hear me? You're breaking up all the time!" shouted Easton into his cell phone as he stood on the deck of the sub.

"Err...I can just about hear you." replied Admiral Berg.

"Where are you sailor?"

"Just approaching Cloudbase 1," uttered Berg, struggling to hold his own cell phone inside his helmet and fly at the same time. He was wobbling badly.

"What's it look like Stig?"

"Massive!"

"Have you made contact with Sam and Spike?"

"Yeah, just now, they've given us instructions for entering the carrier, and they're in position. What are my instructions?"

"Get your boys to disable all of its fighters, disable the flight deck, and take complete control of the ship. We need that ship over this side of the Atlantic!"

"Not too much to do then?" joked Berg as he closed in on the cloudship.

"OK, good luck Stig, the world's counting on you and your boys, we're all behind you. Look, I'm going to have to go, we're diving soon. Keep in touch and as soon as you're in control of Cloudship 1 call me, we'll tell you exactly where you can find the other one."

Within five minutes the USS Springfield was headed down the Potomac River and preparing to dive, whilst the NSA was on the phone to the President telling him of the plan.

Chapter 47

The M JK arrive on board Cloudbase 1.

One by one the thirteen man team climbed into the escape chute and shuffled their way up and along the narrow passageway following Sam Marsh's instructions. One by one they plopped through the opening in the Auxiliary Control Room and met up with Sam and Spike.

"Stig!" said Sam, rushing to give his friend a big hug,

"I'm glad you've come."

"Hi! What is all this Sam, don't you think taking control of a cloudship with just a best friend for help is a big ask even for Sam Marsh the Viking King!" teased Stig as Alfie Blom appeared next, "We thought you might like some help."

"I've got help Stig," replied Sam, pointing to the Robodivers.

"What?" replied Stig, "Where did you get all this lot?" Stig eyed the grubby looking Robodivers suspiciously, "they're a bit, a bit."

"Homemade?" butted in Spike.

"That's because they are," added Sam proudly.

"You are amazing Sam Marsh!" tutted Admiral Stig.

"Did you enjoy the flight, Alfie?" asked Spike.

"Did I ever!" replied the retired Norwegian Admiral, "It's just the best, I thought rocket powered sofa's were neat but these!

We're going to make a fortune out of those suits when we get out of here!"

"If we get out of here," mumbled Spike.

Quickly and professionally Admiral Stig's men took their gear out of their rucksacks (that they'd had to carry on their fronts whilst flying) and methodically prepared the contents. It was mostly high explosive equipment, hundreds of metres of detonation cord (which was specially made plastic wiring full of dynamite), plastic explosives, grenades, and an arsenal of guns, machine guns, rocket and missiles launchers. The weapons were shared out with Robodiver team.

"Do you think your boys could use some of these Zebedee?" asked Stig.

"Affirmative Sir," replied the Robodiver, "Point and fire!"

"That's about it!" replied Morten, "I like these guys!"

Each of the men ditched their flying helmets for black balaclavas and made sure that their ear pieces and radios were working and everyone was on the right, secret frequency. Spike made sure the Robodivers were connected too. They were going to be a vital part of the assault team.

Very soon the soldiers, human and robot were ready to make sure Cloudbase 1 didn't launch any more fighter saucer craft, then they would secure control of the vessel and then they would let Sam, Spike and Alfie take control of the ship itself and fly it across the Atlantic to save America!

Before the dozen commandoes and the dozen Robodivers set off they had a group huddle and did a lot of back patting and hugging, the robots found it strange at first but soon got the hang of it. Then they were ready for action.

"Good luck Stig," called Sam.

"We don't need luck Sam," a familiar voice came through one of the black masks, "the enemy do!"

Stig, four other soldiers and half of the Robodivers set off for the bridge of the Cloudship back through the escape tunnel system, whilst Morten, six men and the other robots set off through the system for the landing deck where they were going to cause complete and utter mayhem.

The landing deck was very quiet with only a small fat man with an extraordinarily large moustache loitering around but he was quickly pounced upon and soon found himself tied up with rope and a large piece of duct tape covering his mouth and moustache. They stuffed him in a small equipment store just off the main deck.

Making sure the security cameras were facing the other way, Morten and a Robodiver ran to the main door control mechanism and stuck a small hunk of explosives into the motor, they then connected up some det cord which they unravelled and joined up to the two main saucer craft elevators that brought up the fighters from the garage hold below. Jasper, one of his men, was already laying explosives in key positions that would ensure the lift wouldn't work for a very long time. Everything was quickly and professionally connected up.

The dozen strange saucer craft that were parked up on the fight deck were entirely wrapped with detonation cord and chunks of plastic explosive were stuck inside any opening they could find. It wouldn't be pretty but it'd be effective.

Some soldiers had gone down to the hangars on the decks below and they too had wired up all the saucer craft with explosives. Very soon everything was ready, connected up and ready to blow.

"Stig can you hear me?" said Morten quietly into his radio.

"I hear you Mort."

"Where are you Chief?"

"Just in the ventilation shaft next to the main bridge. We need to synchronise, I'll put a couple of sonic stun grenades through the grill just as your bonfire starts to go up, then we'll fire in our rubber bullets to take out everyone still conscious on the bridge. The Robodivers are going to sonic blast any droids. We'll go straight in after that and tie everyone up, humans, robots whoever is there! If they don't resist no one will be harmed. Sam is then going to make a broadcast just as soon as we give him the nudge. OK?"

"OK," replied Morten, "Sam, are you Alfie and Spike ready to take control of this thing when we start the party?"

"Yes, we're ready Morten," replied Sam, looking at Spike who gave him the thumbs up, "Spike's logged into their system, he says they're not as clever as they think they are! At your command we're ready to override."

"OK, is everybody safe?" said Morten. By this Morten meant was everyone ready to start doing their respective jobs in order to take control of Cloudship 1.

One by one all the men and Robodivers replied they were.

"OK let's have fun!" said Morten, beginning to count down, "Five, four, three, two, one, bang!"

BANNNNNNNNG! BANNNNNNNNG!BANNNNNNNNG!BANN NNNNNNG!

Mega explosions were rocking the entire flying carrier, Cloudship 1 was under attack from the inside and was completely unprepared.

Within a fraction of a second the immense flight deck was enveloped in balls of fires and explosion after explosion. A wall of fire ten metres across quickly worked its way up the flight deck incinerating everything in its path.

In total precision all the explosions boomed at once all over the cloudship. There were explosions and fires on the flight deck and all the hangar decks.

The doors, the elevators, saucer craft, hangars, the bridge, everything was blowing up. It was like hell itself. Fires burned everywhere and smaller explosions boomed on and on. Everything was white hot, walls were melting around about the MJK men, who were quickly rushing back to the auxiliary control room through the escape tunnels to wait for the sprinkler system and the emergency fire prevention systems to put everything out.

On the bridge, Stig and his men had fired sonic grenades into the large control centre. Then the Robodivers disabled the droids. This was followed up with a hail of rubber bullets and then they stormed the room, tying up humans and robots alike and dragging them quickly and unceremoniously to a secure room. The bridge was badly damaged but Sam, Spike and Alfie were now in control of the ship.

As soon as the men were safely back, Spike made sure all the internal doors in the entire carrier were shut and locked. No one on the entire cloudship was going anywhere. He also blocked any communications links, nobody was going to tell Herr Krater what they'd done either.

Like the genius he was Spike had already shifted control of the ship to the room they were in and locked everyone else out. Now it was Alfie Blom who was flying Cloudship 1.

"Crew members of Cloudship 1," said Sam Marsh over the tannoy, "your vessel is now under the control of Norway. You will not attempt to communicate with The Company, you will not resist us or attempt to interfere with us. Anyone who does will walk the plank!"

"Nice touch Sammy," said Spike nudging his friend.

"Thanks," grinned Sam.

"OK enough joking. Let's go and find us that other cloudship before it blows up America!" said Alfie as everyone watched monitors showing the robot fire brigade of Cloudship 1 putting out all the fires as sprinklers doused everywhere.

"I hope you lot haven't broken everything," said Alfie as all the commandoes appeared one by one and sat down with their bottles of water. The Robodivers preferred to stand.

"Err...I can confirm that they haven't," replied Spike checking his computers, "All the saucer craft are down, but the primary weapon is, is...err," Spike grinned cheekily, "still working!"

"Neat!" grinned Sam, "Here I come Great Grandpa!"

Chapter 48

Cloudbase 2 approaches the White House and prepares its primary weapon.

"Cloudbase 2 is approaching Washington DC and we are ready to fire the primary weapon on your order," said Admiral Schwartz to Herr Krater.

"Let's keep them waiting a little longer," replied Herr Krater, who was sat in the Admiral's chair on the bridge of the cloudship. He wanted to make the administration of the United States of America sweat, "Let them wait, let them tremble. Come down to five thousand feet, I want to see it with my own eyes when we destroy their beloved White House. I want them to see us!"

Slowly, Cloudship 2 started descending. Lower and lower she came until the people of Washington DC could actually see the immense space ship. The deep, low hum of the cloudship was waking people up and they were coming out onto the streets despite requests through the media and by loud speaker announcements for them to stay inside.

Fearing another attack like the one in London the day before, many people gathered what possessions they could and piled their families and pets into their cars to get out of town as quickly as possible.

Soon the roads and highways heading out of Washington DC

were gridlocked. Fuel stations were running out of petrol and there was a dark sense of panic flooding throughout the city.

From his lofty vantage point Herr Krater could see the panic his cloudship was causing on the population of the American capital and he was savouring every moment.

The thirty minute deadline to evacuate the White House came and went, now it had passed by over thirty minutes and the Presidential building was still standing proudly like a beacon in the night, it's stars and stripes flying defiantly from the flag pole.

"Sir, we have a large unidentified aircraft flying towards us across the Atlantic Ocean," reported the Executive Officer.

"A large aircraft?" replied Admiral Schwartz, "*what* large aircraft?"

"We are unable to identify it Sir."

"How is that so?" asked Herr Krater furiously, "We can identify everything!"

"Sorry Sir," continued the XO, "This one we can't. It's closing in on us, fast!"

"I did not know they had this kind of technology, how can my information be so wrong?" For a moment Krater was in a state of utter amazement and unwavering despair.

"Slim, can you hear me?" asked Alfie Blom.

The signal was weak, but the NSA was there, "I hear you Alfie, where are you?"

"We're closing in on the other cloudship."

"He's turning!" shouted Sam, who was sat at the controls.

"He's powering up his primary weapon," reported Spike, checking the computer.

"Can you block it or something Spike?" asked a worried Alfie.

"No, I've tried, I can't."

"Well power up our primary weapon Sam," ordered Alfie.

"Aye, aye, but we won't be ready before he is," replied Sam.

"Alfie, Alfie, are you still there? Can you hear me?" shouted the NSA out of the cell phone.

184

"We hear you Slim, but we're kinda in a spot of bother up here at the moment!"

"Yeah, so I heard, look I might be able to help, give me a few seconds willya!"

"The fewer the better," joked Alfie as all the commandoes looked on nervously.

"Cliff!" The NSA called over to the Massachusetts police man, "Call up your friend willya, what's his name?"

"Leif?"

"Yeah, Leif, call him up please, now! When you get a signal pass the phone to the weapons officer, what's his name? Hoyt, over there."

Cliff quickly started dialling.

The NSA turned to Hoyt, "Hoyt, love the name, by the way, when Cliff's phone connects triangulate the position of the cloudship the phone is on, we'll only have one shot at this so you gotta do it right first time. Feed the coordinates into the patriot system, get those babies fired off at the target you come up with. Aim at the primary weapon! That's vital! Got that sailor?"

"Got it Sir." replied Hoyt, "Triangulate, fire on the primary weapon Sir!" Hoyt didn't have a clue what he was looking for or aiming at, but the NSA seemed certain, and an order was an order.

"It's connected," said Cliff, passing the phone to Hoyt, who immediately connected the cell phone up to his system and went to work.

Five seconds passed.

"How much longer Hoyt?" asked Easton nervously.

"Nearly done," replied Hoyt.

Ten seconds, fifteen.

"Hoyt?" The NSA was getting really worried, "We don't have much time!"

"Done!" replied the sailor, "Co-ordinates are with the patriot team, they're nearly ready, they've..." Hoyt paused, he was watching his system, "fired!"

Two dozen patriot ground to air missiles launched from the White House simultaneously and flew off at over mach four towards Cloudship 2.

As soon as Cloudship 2 saw the patriots coming it re-routed all its power from its primary weapon to its shields but not in time. The shields were only at fifty percent power when one after another the missiles smashed into the vast hull. Herr Krater's invincible Cloudship 2 was under attack.

Lethal Patriots Missiles were slamming into her and the closing Cloudship 1 was arming her primary weapon ready to fire on the enemy.

Within a minute Cloudship 2's shield system and all her fighter shields were only working on part power and worse, her primary weapon had been completely destroyed. She was a lame duck!

"Fire our primary weapon at the flight deck!" ordered Stig Berg, "Stop them launching their fighters!"

"Aye, aye," replied Sam Marsh, "Spike can you set the co-ordinates please?"

"Done it already Sam!"

"Three, two, one!" Sam pressed the fire button and the entire cloudship rocked as the powerful weapon fired a lethal beam of electrical power across the sky and hit its target perfectly.

"Perfect hit Sam," reported Spike checking the sensors.

"We've been hit Sir," replied the XO on Cloudship 2, "badly hit, the flight deck is completely disabled."

"What else?" asked Schwartz, casually glancing over his shoulder towards Herr Krater, but the old man had gone.

"The primary weapon is down and the shields are at fifty percent, just! I don't think they'll stay at that level, we're a sitting target Sir!"

"Climb!" ordered the Admiral, "We need height and lots of it!"

"Course?" asked the XO.

"West, number one!" ordered Schwartz, "Due west and as fast as we can!"

Chapter 49

Herr Krater flees disaster.

Waiting at the very top of Cloudship 2 in a special large deserted hangar was a pitch black spherical object about the size of two storey house.

The old man was hastily pulling on his long winter coat and placing his hat on his head when a small door sized hatch opened in the side of the Orbitsphere.

A familiar grinning figure appeared at the door and came down a small flight of steps to help the old man.

"Vater!" The strange robot called in a metallic voice as the man got closer, his arms were wide open and welcoming.

"RomyRomy! Thank goodness you are here," Krater hugged the robot showing uncharacteristic emotion, "How long have you been waiting here my child?"

"I have just arrived Vater."

Admiral RomyRomy helped Herr Krater up the steps and into the Orbitsphere, then he closed the door and took his position at the helm.

"What are my orders Vater?" he asked.

"I must leave the Earth, Child, take me to my lunar retreat, there is no time to delay."

"Aye, aye, Vater!"

RomyRomy engaged the engines and the round ship floated silently off the launch pad. Up above the round craft the roof of the cloudship's hangar blasted off allowing the ship to shoot out in to the dark night, heading upwards, higher and higher towards the moon.

Chapter 50

Destination, the Grand Canyon!

"She's running away Alfie!" reported Sam.

"That's gotta mean she's disabled!" said Admiral Stig, picking up his phone, "Slim, we've got her, she's disabled, she's fleeing!"

"Follow her!" ordered the NSA from his submarine headquarters, "Follow her and when it's safe, bring her down, don't destroy her if you can manage it and make sure no people on the ground get hurt! Got that Stig?"

"Got it! Will do...Did you hear that everyone?" Stig addressed the entire population of the small auxiliary control room, "We've won!"

A large cheer went up from the men and Robodivers and when it died down, Stig walked over to the controls and spoke quietly to Alfie, Sam and Spike.

"We've got to follow the other cloudship and when it's safe, bring it down but not destroy it, Slim doesn't want us to destroy it, and no one else must be hurt!"

They flew on for well over half an hour chasing the fleeing Cloudship 2.

"She's flying south southwest," reported Sam, "she's got limited power, but the captain certainly knows his stuff! She climbed as high as she could before her power went and now she's starting to slowly lose height so can travel a maximum distance."

"Spike, can you calculate where she's going to eventually come down?" asked Alfie.

Spike did some calculations on the computer and turned ashen faced at everyone.

"Spike!" said Alfie, "What is it Spike?"

"Spike, what is it?" asked Sam.

"I just worked out where it's going to come down," said Spike, who could barely believe what his calculations had come up with. He went through the figures again.

"And?" asked Admiral Stig, getting worried, "Where is it going to come down Spike?"

"You're not going to like this, and neither is Slim!"

"Spike!" shouted everyone.

"The Grand Canyon! Cloudship 2 is going to come down right smack bang in the Grand Canyon unless we do something!"

Alfie glanced back at Stig Berg, Morten Rudd, the other MJK and the Robodivers, "Stig, it's over to you, it's one of the wonders of the world, we can't have this happen there!"

"It's perhaps the best place, mainly uninhabited. Yet I'm sure that landing will kill everyone on board that ship," added Sam, "and remember there are a load of people on board! No offence Zebedee."

"None taken Sir," replied the Robodiver.

Chapter 51

Lives to save, a cloudship to ground safely.

Admiral Stig Berg and his men had taken part in lots of missions, most of them deadly but they'd never used angel suits to fly from one cloudship to another to try and save hundreds of lives and leave the reputation and perhaps beauty of one of the wonders of the world intact.

"You need to get on board and get to the auxiliary control room." said Spike, "Plug in this, it's Sam's iPhone and dial up my number, it's on the speed dial. As soon as we get a connection...and I hope there is a signal, I'll try and control Cloudship 2 from here."

"OK." replied Stig. The Admiral trusted Spike, he thought the boy had a lot of talent, certainly more than him when it came to computers.

Stig and his men had put their helmets back on and stowed their weapons back in their backpacks. The Robodivers readied themselves too.

"Come on men, robots let's go!" shouted Morten.

"Hey!" called Sam after them, "You can't use those guns, people could get killed! Here! Look what I've found down here!"

Sam had opened a small closet in the auxiliary control room which was full of strange looking rifles.

"What've you got there Sam?" asked Stig.

"Guns," replied Sam, picking one up and waving it about.

ZZZZZZZZZZZZZZZZ! A green laser beam shot out of the end.

"SAM!" yelled everyone ducking down.

"Err, sorry!" mumbled Sam, lowering the weapon.

"I think we'll take some of them," said Morten delving into the cupboard and bringing out a load of the guns, "Come on everyone, drop your automatics and each grab a couple of these beauties!"

"You can set them to stun!" discovered Sam.

"Yeah, we can!" added Admiral Stig.

One by one the men and Robodivers climbed into the emergency life pod tunnel and disappeared out of sight.

"Good luck!" called Sam, Spike and Alfie all together after them.

"Thanks," replied Stig as he disappeared, the last one to go, "We need it!"

Chapter 52

Boarding Cloudbase 2, The MJK take control!
Leif Ericson and Spug Myers help.

The Robodivers took to flying like ducks to water but it had taken the men a bit longer. But by now the men of the elite MJK were expert flyers. It was like second nature to them. One by one they crawled out along the emergency exit chutes on Cloudship 1 and out of the exit hatch, which Spike had opened for them.

It took no time at all to get over to the other ship and by the time they boarded Cloudship 2, Spike had told them he would have opened another hatch in exactly the same position as the one they'd left on Cloudship 1.

"What?" shouted Admiral Berg as he gripped onto the side of the huge ship.

"What is it, Sir?" replied Morten.

"The hatch isn't open, Spike's failed!"

"Let's open it the old fashioned way!" grinned Morten. There was no time to be subtle and they knew that the systems on board the stricken ship would probably alert the crew to their arrival as soon the hatch was blasted open but the MJK had no choice.

"Zebedee, lace up the explosives!" called Admiral Stig.

The cloudships were flying fast and high, though they were losing height all the time. They were flying perilously close, only a couple of miles apart. Alfie, Sam and Stig were proving excellent pilots and were able to hold number one at a perfect distance.

Zebedee placed some plastic explosives on the door and used a few metres of det cord, everyone quickly took cover and then he blew it. The hatch flew off dramatically and everyone climbed in.

One by one the commandos edged their way up the narrow channels until they were up to the grill.

"All clear," whispered Morten to the other and he braced himself to kick the door open. Smash! The door flew in.

ZZZZZZZZZZZZZZZZ! A laser gun fired at Morten.

"Ah!" he yelled, grabbing his shoulder.

ZZZZZZZZZZZZZZZZ! More firing.

Two soldiers pulled their captain back inside and back along the tunnel where first aid was administered.

ZZZZZZZZZZZZZZZZZ!   ZZZZZZZZZZZZZZZZZ! ZZZZZZZZZZZZZZZZ! ZZZZZZZZZZZZZZZZZ! ZZZZZZZZZZZZZZZZZ! ZZZZZZZZZZZZZZZZZ!

The commandoes returned fire with interest! Quickly the Robodivers leapt passed and fired their weapons wildly all around the room.

"All clear!" called Zebedee.

Now the auxiliary control room was all quiet. The men looked inside and discovered that a maintenance robot had taken a direct hit from the Robodivers and was now lying motionless on the floor.

"All clear," they shouted.

As more men came into the room they dragged Morten with them and laid him on the floor. He'd lost a lot of blood and looked terrible.

"I'm fine, I'm fine!" he grumbled.

A first aid Robodiver quickly administered first aid, stopped the bleeding and sat with Morten.

At the auxiliary controls Stig connected up the iPhone and dialled up Spike's number.

"It's ringing!" he said, sighing with relief.

Thankfully there was a strong signal and Spike was able to log into Cloudbase 2's control system.

The commandoes filed out of the room and started scouring the ship for the hostages. As they worked methodically they met heavy resistance at first and the going was painfully slow. But they were experts in this kind of close quarter combat and the Robodivers were quick learners, following the actions of the men closely. The human and robot crew of the cloudship were not in the same league as the commandos. All the laser weapons of the MJK were set to stun but they'd anticipated that those of the crew would be set to kill!

The bridge was the scene of the hardest fighting, the crew were waiting for them and well dug in, yet the soldiers were used to this kind of close combat.

"I want to speak with the Admiral!" ordered Berg as his men set off stun grenades.

Smoke filled the bridge and the executive officer was desperately trying to regain control of the cloudship.

Berg fired his laser and took the XO out, ZZZZZZZZZZZZZZZ! Someone shot Stig's arm.

"Argh!" yelled Berg returning fire.

ZZZZZZZZZZZZZZZZ!   ZZZZZZZZZZZZZZZZ! ZZZZZZZZZZZZZZZZ! ZZZZZZZZZZZZZZZZ! ZZZZZZZZZZZZZZZZ! ZZZZZZZZZZZZZZZZ!

Someone was now coming onto the bridge and firing ferociously!

"I'll give you tin heads some more of that too!" yelled big Leif Erickson who was firing like a man possessed, "Stealing ma boat like that! Aint gonna let no one steal ma boat. It's Leif Erickson's ship! Take that!!"

196

ZZZZZZZZZZ! ZZZZZZZZZ!

"Have some for Spug Wilson too!" yelled the astronaut angrily as he followed Erickson into the room.

"Mr Erickson!" yelled Stig.

"Err...what? Yeah?"

"Mr Erickson! Mr Wilson!" he yelled again, "We're the good guys! Norwegian Commandos! Can you stop firing? We've already got control of the bridge!"

ZZZZZZZZZZZZZZZZZ! "Not quite!" yelled Admiral Schwartz opening fire on Stig, who was already injured.

ZZZZZZZZZZZZZZZZZ!   ZZZZZZZZZZZZZZZZZ! ZZZZZZZZZZZZZZZZZ! ZZZZZZZZZZZZZZZZZ! ZZZZZZZZZZZZZZZZZ! ZZZZZZZZZZZZZZZZ!

Leif Erickson and Spug Wilson blasted the Admiral!

"Now we have!" they yelled triumphantly.

Chapter 53

Escape to the Moon

The Orbitsphere ship was rocketing out of the Earth's powerful grasp and into a high orbit above the planet.

"Ah...It does look strangely peaceful from up here," sighed Herr Krater looking down, "what do you think my child?"

"Very blue!" replied RomyRomy, "Very blue indeed. Are you ready to commence lunar catapult, Vater?"

Herr Krater sighed again, "I am ready." He was looking at an English newspaper clipping from the Yorkshire Post Newspaper, it was titled "Sam Marsh the Viking King moves to start a new life on Norwegian Islands. "He's a clever young man, that Sam Marsh," admitted Krater quietly.

"Who is Sam Marsh?" asked RomyRomy curiously.

Krater ignored the question.

"Who is Sam Marsh?" repeated the droid.

"My Great Grandson," said Krater quietly.

"Ah."

"Now, let us go and see what progress Professor Jahnke is making!"

Expertly, Admiral RomyRomy engaged the lunar catapult, which used the magnetic field of the Earth and the round ship zoomed around the entire circumference of the planet three times getting faster and faster before firing off towards the moon at maximum velocity.

Chapter 54

Aftermath, peace restored to Washington and
London.

"**A**mazing scenes here over the skies of Washington DC in the early hours of this morning," reported the BBC news correspondent on the BBC world service channel that was blaring out in the office of the NSA in the West Wing of the White House. Nobody was watching the scenes as everyone was stood about chatting and eating a well earned breakfast.

"Nice work there boys!" said Slim Easton, patting Sam Marsh and Spike Williams on the back. He was laughing. "However, next time you decide to set off and fight some bad guys on your own, make sure you've got the help you need actually with you!"

"We had our soldiers!" replied Sam.

"Yeah I heard about that Sam! Building your own Robodivers and from junk too! Well done. Still, take some adults with you next time!"

"We will Sir," the boys replied together.

"Err Sir?" asked Sam quietly, "Can I ask you a question?"

"Sure! Fire away!" replied the NSA.

"What's happened to the cloudships?"

"Aw, not much really," mumbled Slim Easton.

"They've taken them on yonder!" butted in Leif Erickson who was enjoying telling everyone of how he was captured and fought a dozen robots before being stunned by a laser gun.

"Yonder?" asked Sam.

"Yeah! They've taken them on yonder, to Nevada!"

Slim Easton coughed and nodded hard at Cliff Marriot to come and shut the big fisherman up.

"To Nevada?" Sam didn't know what he was talking about.

"To that there secret base in the desert that they try and tell everyone doesn't exist!"

"Oh.." said Sam suddenly realising what Erickson was talking about , "...you mean Area 51? They've taken them to Area 51? Is that where you've taken them Mr Easton?"

"I'm afraid that information is classified," replied the NSA formally.

"No it aint!" continued Leif who was in full flow, "It aint classified and it aint a secret base, Mr Easton, everyone knows it's there, by golly, we all watch documentaries about it on the TV every evening!"

"Would you like some more scrambled eggs, Leif?" butted in Marriot, pushing Erickson to one side and away from the NSA and his guests.

"Well, I hear you're joining the US Navy real soon Spike?" injected Slim Easton changing the subject.

"Oh yes, yes Sir, three years in September, Sir, but

I'm spending the whole summer at Annapolis," replied Spike standing to attention, "thank you."

Annapolis is the home to the United States Naval Academy. Spike had been invited to spend every summer until he became sixteen at the academy, learning about life in the US Navy, though everyone knew Spike would end up working with military development rather than become an actual sailor.

"And what about you Sam," asked Easton, "have you got any plans for the future?"

"Well I don't know yet, I hadn't really thought about it," replied Sam who was still getting used to the fact that he wasn't an orphan from a council estate in Holmford, Yorkshire, England, but had a life and history in the Lofoten Islands.

"Stop trying to steal him from us!" interrupted Alfie Blom, "He's ours, you can't have him Slim Easton, he's Norwegian, the Chieftain of Lofoten, Sam Marsh is the Viking King and he's got some islands to manage!"

"OK, OK I promise not to steal him..." joked the NSA, "...but we might have to borrow him from time to time if that's OK."

"I'm sure that would be OK," laughed Alfie, who stopped laughing when he saw Sam's expression, "Sam, what's the matter?"

"Oh, I was just worried about Stig and Morten."

"Don't worry about them Sam, they're like rubber men! They all are, the MJK, they're indestructible, look, they're here now!"

Admiral Stig and Morten appeared at the door, well bandaged and strapped up but grinning from ear to ear.

"Sam!" they yelled, waiving.

"You won't believe what we've arranged to fly you home in?" added Stig grinning.

"Not a cloudship 'cos they've gone to Area 51!" yelled Leif, before a hefty security guard asked him politely to shut up divulging national secrets!

"What?" asked Sam, who was suddenly feeling really exhausted.

"Concorde!" yelled Morten.

"Concorde!" replied Sam, "That's not possible, they're all out of service."

"Not all of them," said Stig, winking, "come on let's not keep her waiting, we want to get home to Norway for tea! I think Jorunn will have made something special!"

"Concorde?" repeated Sam, "Are you sure?"

"Sure we are!"

Chapter 55

Flying Concorde to the Lofoten celebrations

S at silently and majestically on the tarmac at Washington Dulles International Airport, forty miles away from downtown DC, was Sam and Spike's dream plane, the most stunningly beautiful aircraft ever built... Concorde. Long and sleek and the now the property of the Norwegian government she was quite small by the standards of other aircrafts and miniscule by the enormous cloudships standards. But she was undoubtedly the most beautiful aircraft either of the plane-mad boys had ever seen! The shape, the sleek lines, to the sharp nose and the powerful boxy engines. To the boys she was completely magnificent.

Sam and Spike had loved everything about planes ever since they were tiny children. When Sam had been really small, Sarah, his social worker had taken him to Leeds Airport to see a visiting Air France Concorde arrive in Yorkshire. He was so small he couldn't remember it that well but he did remember his chest vibrating and his head had felt like exploding as the long bird rumbled in out of a cloud filled sky.

Now Concorde was here! It was like a dream come true! They were so excited to be actually flying in the most famous plane ever built that they could barely bring themselves to speak.

"Hi Sam! Hi Spike!" The sound of two female voices was calling from the top of the high steps that led up to the body of the plane.

Grinning down at the boys were two familiar smiling faces, the beautiful stewardesses Anita and Hilde.

"Hilde? Anita?" said Sam, gobsmacked!

"Come on up boys!" called Hilde, "Captain Harket is keen to fly Concorde."

"Captain Harket is here too?" Spike grinned to Sam.

"Looks like it, come on Spike, come on everybody!"

The two boys ran up the steep stairs and were followed by the MJK team and Alfie, the Robodivers, who had to almost crawl through the small door and last but not least the very weary Stig and Morten.

"After take-off you can both go and sit up in the cockpit," said Anita.

As soon as Captain Harket gave the order Sam and Spike wouldn't need telling twice.

"God dag!" said the Captain in Norwegian, who then continued in English, "This is Captain Harket speaking to you this morning. Welcome to Concorde! Hello Sam and Spike, you are our special guests on this royal flight to Svolvaer this morning. We will, of course be flying supersonic today, and with a flight ceiling of 59,000 feet planned, I expect the journey time for a distance to the Norwegian Lofoten Islands of around 3700 miles to take two hours forty five minutes."

"Hey! It should be quicker than that?" mumbled Sam to no one in particular, yet Captain Harket hadn't finished.

"...this length of time is due to supersonic flight restrictions and take-off and landing Sam."

"Oh..." said Sam looking around, but no one was listening.

"Please fasten seatbelts," said Anita and Hilde, walking up and down the narrow centre aisle, it was very cramped but no one cared about that, "please fasten your seatbelt...please fasten your seatbelt...Admiral Berg, excuse me, please fasten your seatbelt."

"Oh, sorry," muttered Stig fastening his seatbelt.

Quickly the two glamorous ladies rushed to their seats at the front and the back of the passenger compartment as the engines started rumbling.

Louder and louder the engines growled until suddenly Concorde set off, not at a run like a normal jet, but at a real sprint until she reached her take off speed of 250 miles per hour! She tilted slightly and then lifted effortlessly off American soil for the first time in nearly a decade. Under the expert control of Captain Harket the thrusters immediately kicked in and the rumbling turned into a roar as the elegant plane soared into the wintery New Year sky. The next stop, Svolvaer, Norway and the real start of the year celebration.

THE END (for now!)
Rob Bullock May 2011

Sam Marsh will return in

"Sam Marsh and the Lunar War".

Excerpt

Saturday June 13th 1943, 3.47 GMT, Lunar Mine S4D, The Daedalus Crater, the Far side of the Moon.

Boom! Boom!Boom!Boom!

Mining the moon was going exceptionally well, the lunar rock was proving easy to hew and it was full of valuable precious minerals like diamonds, bauxite and nickel.

"Do you know? This small insignificant satellite will win us the war Jahnke!" said Herr Krater, surveying the sub lunar activity with great pride, "They don't have a clue how we are able to meet the challenges of almost the entire world because they don't know our secret. They don't even know that we're even up here on the moon. Pathetic idiots!"

"This is so true," replied Herr Krater's trusty sidekick.

"Argh!" screamed a miner from the rock face far below, "Argh!" he screamed again.

Jahnke's radio crackled to life, "Professor Jahnke Schmidt is dead." The voice was panicky and scared, "Something killed him!"

"Repeat what you just said man!" shouted the professor into his radio.

"Something killed Schmidt! Oh no, no, no, argh!!!!!!"

"What the? Hello! Hello! Operative come in!" called Jahnke who turned to Krater, "It's happening again Sir!"

"Nonsense!" replied Krater, "It's probably just another lunar accident that's all!"

"But you heard the man!"

"I heard nothing of the sort!"

"Herr Sturmbannfuhrer! I suggest we evacuate this site immediately until it can be made safe and the dragons contained!" pleaded Jahnke to his commander.

"Request denied," replied Krater coldly, waiving his hand dismissively and walking back to his Earth bound shuttle, "seal this mine up, gather the operation up and move to another site elsewhere on the dark side of the moon. We have no time to waste! There's a war to be won man."

OKANAGAN PUBLIC LIBRARY
3 3132 03388 6997

CPSIA information can be obtained at www.ICGtesting.com
Printed in the USA
LVOW040944050812

292976LV00005B/47/P